FORBIDDEN FLOWERS

An embarrassing slip in the Hyde Park mud leads Lily and Rose Banister into the path of Phillip Montgomery, a British Embassy diplomat. Mesmerised by Lily's beauty, he invites her to accompany him to the Paris Exhibition, while Rose, who can't help but feel envious, is asked to chaperone the trip. Arriving in Paris, the trio happen upon Phillip's old adversary Gordon Pomfret, who decides to join their group, obviously vying for Lily's attention. Meanwhile, Rose and Phillip discover that their shared interests might just make them kindred spirits . . .

ALICE ELLIOTT

FORBIDDEN FLOWERS

Complete and Unabridged

LINFORD
Leicester

First published in Great Britain in 2019

First Linford Edition
published 2020

A catalogue record for this book is available
from the British Library.

ISBN 978–1–4448–4458–0

Published by
Ulverscroft Limited
Anstey, Leicestershire

Set by Words & Graphics Ltd.
Anstey, Leicestershire
Printed and bound in Great Britain by
T. J. International Ltd., Padstow, Cornwall

This book is printed on acid-free paper

A Slip in the Mud

'Oh, Rose, look!' Lily Banister squealed as she spotted a parade of soldiers marching in sequence across Hyde Park one Wednesday afternoon. 'Let's go and watch them.'

Before Rose knew it, her younger sister had flown across the grass in a flash of dove white. Her pale skirts which were patterned with tiny violet flowers fluttered in the light breeze.

The temperature was pleasant for March even though it had rained all morning. Rose watched as Lily darted past the trees. She was remarkably fast given the length of her fine skirts and petticoats.

'Lily, be careful,' Rose warned, although her sister was now out of earshot. The sun was shining but there was still lots of mud around from the morning's downpour.

Lily had already squelched through a couple of boggy patches on the grass. Her delicate white shoes would need a thorough clean when they got home and the hem of her dress dangled precariously above the sodden grass.

Rose took her time as she walked the long way round and made sure she stuck to the paths. Wherever Lily went, calamity usually followed. At least one of them had to be sensible.

'Quickly, slow coach,' Lily called. 'You're missing it all.' The soldiers had come to a halt in front of the small crowd that had gathered to watch. The drummers continued to beat as the soldiers saluted the crowd.

Just then a tall, distinguished gentleman appeared. He wore a smart thick lounging jacket despite the spring sunshine, and a top hat. His mind appeared to be elsewhere for he stood right in front of the ladies, utterly eclipsing their view.

'Drat,' Lily muttered, as she tried to take a few steps to the other side, but unfortunately yet more people had joined the crowd and any movement risked getting far closer to them than would have been fitting for a lady.

Lily then resorted to taking tiny jumps in the air.

Rose heard the 'squeak' and then the 'squelch' of Lily's white shoes as she landed slightly awkwardly from one of her jumps. Wobbling and out of control, Lily grabbed her sister's arm to try to steady herself, but it was too late.

Rose winced as Lily let go and fell backwards on to the soggy grass below, narrowly missing a young couple who were standing behind them. They hastily moved out of the way.

'Rose, quickly.' Lily's face was aghast as Rose leaned down to take her arm again and haul her up. Both sisters were in a state of shock. The whole thing had happened so quickly.

The back of Lily's white and violet dress was drenched in muddy water. It clung to every inch of the material and was dripping from her petticoats like rain from guttering.

Her hat, which was fashionably topped with soft pale feathers to match her dress, was mercifully unharmed, but it now sat at a jaunty angle on her comely round face, which was usually so bright and cheerful.

'Goodness, miss, are you hurt?' The distinguished gentleman who had blocked their view had turned around and was looking at Lily in concern. Her tumble had clearly jolted him from whatever daydream he'd been swept up in before.

Rose noticed that he had expressive hazel eyes. He was clean shaven, too. Although she knew little of the fashions of the day, Rose was fairly sure Lily would say that this gent was following the 1860s trends. She made sure she was well informed on such matters.

'Thank you, sir, but I'm perfectly well.' Lily's voice which was usually so full of laughter was now tight and clipped, plus her face told a different story. Her blue eyes were bright with tears and her cheeks were flushed far pinker than even Lily, who loved her new rouge, would ever want them to be.

'Come, Rose, we really must go home,' Lily went on. She hadn't let go of her sister's arm and was now pulling it much tighter than Rose felt was necessary.

'Would you permit me to call on you later to check you are fully recovered?' The gentleman wasn't ready to let go yet. 'Allow me to introduce myself. My name is Phillip Montgomery.'

'Oh, that won't be necessary,' Lily started, but for once, Rose's voice was louder than hers.

'We would be delighted, Phillip,' she answered firmly, reaching into her purse for one of her cards. 'We are Misses Rose and Lily Banister,' she added as he took it.

Phillip raised his top hat in farewell, revealing thick wavy dark hair in a side-parting. Rose inclined her head in a genteel bow, but Lily had already turned away. The parade had finished now and the crowds were dispersing anyway.

'Keep close behind me, Rose,' Lily hissed as her sister hurried to follow her. 'I don't want people to see the mess I'm in. Whatever were you thinking inviting that man to call on us? It was all his fault in the first place and surely I'm humiliated enough!'

'Oh, Lily, we don't even know that he will,' Rose replied. 'Plus it would have been both improper and impolite to decline his suggestion.' Thankfully Lily was too determined to arrive home without anyone of their acquaintance seeing her to argue further with her sister.

'Let's just try and get upstairs without upsetting Mama,' she said. They both knew how Mrs Banister would react on seeing the state of Lily's dress. The ordeal was best avoided.

It wasn't long before the sisters reached their family home, a tall and pleasant town-house on Upper Wimpole Street, Marylebone.

Nell, the Banisters' housemaid, had come to the door and after a hurried exchange of frantic whispers, Rose and Lily galloped up the stairs whilst Nell got to work on heating the water for a bath.

Lily then retreated into her bedroom, accompanied by Rose, and changed out of the sodden clothes. The mud had soaked through to her petticoat, but mercifully her expensive hooped crinoline remained unscathed.

'She doesn't seem to have noticed,' Lily remarked. She had begun to recover. Rose noticed that a ghost of a smile had returned to her lips and her cheeks had returned to their regular shade of pink. Relieving herself of the soggy and stained garments had instantly put her in a better humour.

Rose was just about to agree when both sisters started and exchanged a look of mutual anguish. Furious and thumping steps were pounding along the landing.

'A bath, at this hour, Lily?' Mrs

Banister thundered as she appeared at the door. 'And, what, pray, was that rumpus earlier? Nell is scurrying around like a shy little rabbit with her head down and won't meet my eye. May I remind you that my servant works for me, not you.'

With her broad shoulders and furrowed brow, Elizabeth Banister was an imposing presence. Her long grey skirts and crisp white blouse gave her a look of a stern headmistress.

She walked right into the bedroom and stood by the cast iron fireplace with her hands on her hips. An angry vein throbbed at her temple.

'Be calm, Mama,' Lily replied somewhat insolently as she sat down on the golden silk stool in front of her dressing table. Rose, who had always been quite intimidated by their mother, was never quite sure how her younger sister held her nerve.

'Explain yourself, child,' Mrs Banister answered.

'At one and twenty, I'm hardly a

8

child,' Lily sang in return. 'I had a slip in the mud, Mama,' she went on. 'In this damp weather it really could have happened to anyone.'

'Gracious heavens!' Mrs Banister sighed, her imposing figure drooped and she sank into a nearby armchair. Her breaths became unnaturally loud and laboured and she placed a hand to her chest. 'In town, I presume? What will everyone think? A Banister daughter sprawling around in the dirt. The shame!'

'It was the edge of Hyde Park,' Lily replied, clearly improvising. 'I don't think anyone of our acquaintance saw and Rose did a capital job of shrouding me from view as we made our way home.'

Rose perched on the edge of her sister's bed as she listened to Lily giving a highly condensed and somewhat rose-tinted version of the afternoon's events.

Slowly their mother's breathing returned to normal and the worst of the storm appeared to pass. It wasn't long before Lily began to chirp about the new dress she should buy to replace the spoiled one.

'You shall do no such thing, young lady,' Mrs Banister said. Her colour was beginning to rise again. 'It was bought this season and has plenty of life in it left. I'll tell Nell to bring washing day a few days forward. As long as you haven't ripped the fabric, it stands a good chance of being wearable once more.'

Lily pouted in annoyance.

'The fashions have changed again, Mama,' she said. '1869 is the year of pizazz. I read it in 'The World Of Fashion' last week.'

'Heavens, you young ladies really mustn't believe everything you read in those magazines,' Mrs Banister replied, rolling her eyes.

'It's true,' Lily went on. 'Emerald green, magenta and azuline blue are the colours we need.'

'So garish,' Mrs Banister murmured.

'If we don't keep ahead of fashions, we'll end up looking like servants,' Lily said, appealing to her mother's social concerns.

It was the custom for ladies to hand down last season's dresses to their maids as gifts, so one could never be quite sure of a girl's social class if she wore anything other than the latest trends.

'And you two will go into service if you spend all our money, Lily,' Mrs Banister said, throwing up her arms in frustration and leaving the room.

As a respectable middle-class family, Rose and her family were uncomfortably aware of the struggles of the lower echelons and, worst still, those who had fallen on ruin.

It was preferable, of course, to stick to the west of the city and the more genteel areas of town. Nevertheless the poverty of the East End could hardly be ignored.

The plight of the less fortunate crept into Rose's conscience and she generally pilfered a couple of potatoes and sometimes some surplus cuts off their Sunday joints and packaged them up to pass on discreetly to families in need on the city streets.

Her parents would not have approved as they worried about her falling in with the 'wrong sort'. They also spent a fair amount of time fretting over their own finances.

Only last week they had come across a lady who had once lived a few doors away selling violets on the street. They were living through hard times and the balance between respectability and ruin had never felt so fragile.

Still, Mr Banister's job at the bank was stable enough and whilst Rose knew that her mother would have liked an extra maid, even Mrs Banister had to concede that life could be an awful lot worse.

Her main focus now was the future of her daughters.

At three and twenty and still unmarried, Rose knew that her likely fate would be to work as a governess.

Mrs Banister had already started giving her titbits of advice, thinly disguised as mere small talk and maternal generosity.

'Rose, dear, I saw this beautiful silver hairbrush on sale in Harrods this afternoon day and immediately thought of you.'

She'd placed a paper bag in Rose's hands.

'Thank you, Mama.' Rose had been surprised. It was unusual for her mother to give her a gift of any kind and it wasn't a special occasion.

'It's a useful thing to have,' Mrs Banister said. 'It sets you apart as a member of our class. They say to governesses, you know, to be sure to place a silver-backed hairbrush or looking glass very visibly in her quarters to show the other servants that she is of a different station to them.'

Rose had thought that might be quite a lonely place to be, and rather isolating. Still, the only other option she could think of was working as a milliner and of the two, a governess was by far the better option.

She had adored the gentle charm of their own governess, Miss Pritchard, and had lapped up her teaching hungrily, relishing every moment.

Rose had a firm understanding of the Classics now, played the piano well and could speak fluent French.

She spent time with Nell every day, too, during any spare moments Mrs Banister allowed her, and had already significantly improved her literacy. She read to Nell whenever she could. They both loved the work of Jane Austen.

The thought of transferring this learning to younger minds wasn't altogether unappealing but, Rose knew how much she would miss her family and home, especially Lily, whom she loved dearly despite her impulsive nature.

The whole prospect of leaving home really was very frightening. Still, she had the beginnings of a plan in her head. It wasn't anything she had spoken of yet, not to anyone, but an idea was there and kept returning to her mind.

Lily had giggled and fidgeted her way through all the lessons and had barely taken in anything at all, but somehow the Banisters didn't fear for their younger daughter in quite the same way.

She was exceptionally beautiful and, of the two Banister sisters, stood the better chance of making a good marriage.

It did seem ironic, Rose thought to herself, that the one time a distinguished gentleman, clearly of high social standing had shown an interest in them, was also the day Lily had disgraced herself in public and was now doing her utmost to pretend the event hadn't taken place at all.

'Well thank goodness that chap didn't turn up,' Lily said as Rose brushed out her flaxen locks with the new silver brush as they prepared for bed.

'His name is Phillip,' Rose replied.

'And what makes you think he won't come tomorrow?'

'Oh, he would have called by this afternoon if he was coming at all,' Lily said breezily. 'I'm sure of it.'

★ ★ ★

It was only after Nell had finished pouring the morning coffee the next day and the last of the breakfast plates had been cleared away, that there was a knock on the Banisters' front door.

Humble Beginnings

Phillip Montgomery had woken that morning at his parents' town house in Kensington Church Street having decided for certain that he would be making his way over to Marylebone to make a call on the Banister sisters that day.

He had spent the previous afternoon and evening in two minds on whether it was a good idea. The look on the younger sister's face had been far from inviting, but there was something about her skin, delicate like porcelain, that he couldn't quite remove from his mind. Her eyes were piercing, too, like newly glazed glass.

'You're quiet this morning, Phillip,' his mother commented over breakfast. 'Are you quite well?'

'Perfectly well, Mama,' Phillip replied, taking a gulp of coffee. In truth, he was very nervous about his call on the Misses Banister.

His role as a diplomat in the British Embassy in Paris required an outward display of confidence, wit and tenacity, but it was remarkable how unsteady he felt now he was back on home soil. His surroundings may have been familiar, but making calls on young ladies was most definitely uncharted territory for him.

Though, perhaps, he reasoned with himself, Miss Banister shares your sense of trepidation and your anxieties over what society might think. The spots of colour in those otherwise flawless cheeks and the way her eyes darted fitfully from side to side, as she recovered from her fall made Phillip feel he may have found a fellow anxious soul.

'Right, Mama,' Phillip said as he drained the last of his morning coffee and scraped his chair back. 'I'm out to take the morning air.'

'I'd join you but I was really quite

restless last night and didn't sleep at all well,' his mother replied, retiring to her chaise longue by the bay windows. 'The cough from my recent cold has really lingered and bothers me most at night.'

Having picked up his lounging jacket and his top hat, Phillip set off down Kensington Church Street, weaving his way around busy passers-by.

There were traders selling fruit and vegetables, plus coffee carts and ladies gliding along in their vast crinoline skirts. The air, heavy with coal smoke and soot, smelled of horses and toasted bread.

Such was his focus on his call that it didn't occur to him until he reached Hyde Park that his mother was spending increasingly long hours indoors, complaining of fatigue, yet struggling to sleep at night.

Phillip felt a pang of guilt and resolved to buy her a bouquet of flowers on the way home. Some daffodils, he thought, as he passed yellow clumps of them in the park.

They would add a splash of sunshine to her sitting-room window.

Phillip knew how much she had been looking forward to his trip home from Paris.

With his father, William Montgomery, so taken up with the family business, a large drapers and haberdashery on Oxford Street, now branching out into quality foodstuffs, perfumery, accessories, Phillip might have worried that his mother was becoming a little isolated, if it wasn't for her small army of friends who would regularly drop by for luncheon and afternoon tea out at Claridges or the new Grosvenor Hotel in Victoria.

Mrs Montgomery also had their trip to Paris to anticipate as well. Phillip was to spend the last of his leave from the embassy back in France.

Firstly, they would be attending one of the great Paris exhibitions, which was taking place during the spring and summer of 1869. It followed the success of a similar event in 1867 which

Phillip hadn't been able to attend due to his heavy workload at the embassy.

He was still disappointed to have missed it and attending this second event would go some way towards making up for it.

They were to travel to the French Rivera afterwards and enjoy a holiday in Nice. Phillip was hopeful that a change of scenery would prove the tonic his mother needed.

Speaking of flowers, he'd better buy a bunch now to take to the Banisters. It wouldn't do to turn up empty handed. He stopped by an upmarket florist at Marble Arch.

'Just the one, sir?' the woman asked as he chose a bouquet of tulips, peonies and daffodils.

'Um . . . ' Phillip hesitated for a second. There were two Miss Banisters so would it be improper to arrive with only one bouquet? Still, it may well look too exuberant to bring two. He was making a call to the household after all, and the flowers were a gift to everyone.

'That's right.' He nodded as he reached into his jacket pocket for some money.

He had reached Marylebone now and was getting closer and closer to Upper Wimpole Street where the Banister sisters lived. The walk had taken close to an hour and Phillip stopped at a nearby bench for a brief rest, to catch his breath and compose his thoughts.

Perhaps he should have caught the omnibus but it wasn't raining and he was quite glad of the exercise. It helped suppress the nerves. The weather was cooler than yesterday and the wind retained a wintry chill but Phillip was warm from walking and barely felt it at all.

'Come on, man!' he murmured to himself as he rose from the bench to resume his journey.

Phillip couldn't quite believe how apprehensive he felt. He tried looking back on previous times in his life when he had started something new and felt those fluttering first-time worries.

He had survived his first day at Eton, for instance, and after that his first day at Oxford University and, most recently, his first day at the British Embassy, when he had started, five years ago, as an unpaid 'attaché', rather like an apprentice diplomat.

He remembered the false joviality in his voice on both occasions as he shook hands and exchanged pleasantries with his peers. Shouldn't it be easier now he was six and twenty and fully fledged as a gentleman and diplomat?

He was, as his mother had informed him only the other week, a highly eligible bachelor. Yet still, Phillip could feel his heart racing beneath his starched shirt and waistcoat and he raised his pocket handkerchief to wipe a bead of sweat from his brow, despite the chilly weather.

The truth was, although Phillip had flourished at school and in his career so far, he wasn't terribly good at getting along with other people.

It wasn't for want of effort.

At school, he had tried hard to fit in. He had joined the cricket team despite not particularly caring for the sport and spent endless hours trying to perfect his bowling skills to do the team proud.

He had even landed himself in trouble a couple of times to impress the others. Notably when he placed a live toad on the French teacher's desk. It had been Gordon Pomfret's idea, of course — he had dared him to do it.

Phillip didn't mention that when the head teacher had caned him in front of the whole school, though deep down he knew Pomfret wouldn't have extended any of that loyalty to him.

It hadn't been easy, coming from what Pomfret and his friends called 'new money'. William Montgomery had started his store with a small loan from the bank and the proceeds of a very small inheritance left for him by an elderly and unmarried aunt. A mixture of good fortune and tireless graft over the following ten years had resulted in the thriving business he owned now.

By the time Phillip had reached his eleventh year, there was ample money to pay for the very best of educations, though, thanks to Eton's young elite, Phillip could never quite forget his roots. He would always be the 'shopkeeper's boy' to them, a joke that odious Pomfret still delighted in repeating several times a day in the embassy office, generally known amongst diplomats as the chancery.

Pomfret had an insufferable habit of calling Phillip 'Monty' too, a nickname he'd always disliked. It had been five years and still, Phillip couldn't quite believe that Pomfret had followed him into the diplomatic service and that they had both ended up at the embassy in Paris, though naturally, as far as Pomfret was concerned, it had been Phillip who had followed him. This leave had proved some welcome respite from that lout of a man.

Phillip could feel his heart rate rising. It wouldn't do to think of Pomfret at a time like this. No, the beast was happily spending his leave engaging in hunting, shooting and fishing at his family's country residence in Kent and never missed an opportunity to boast about his flamboyant lifestyle at home.

He certainly wouldn't be ruminating about Phillip. If anything, all he would feel was the occasional burst of smug satisfaction at his success in his goading of Phillip, especially if he knew how annoyed Phillip was by the mere thought of him.

Phillip stopped by a shoe shiner and flicked the boy a farthing for a quick polish. He was nearly there now.

'Come on, Montgomery,' he whispered to himself, 'you're a successful diplomat with good prospects and are of good social standing. Just remember to act like it.'

'I'm finished now, mister,' the shiner said a few minutes later. 'You was miles away!' It took Phillip a moment to register that the boy was talking to him.

'True,' Phillip murmured, throwing

the lad an extra penny for a tip. The boy's grubby face was drawn, tight and hungry looking. You didn't have to look far to find poverty in London. It stared you out from behind street corners, hissed at you in the murky air and tapped you on the shoulder when your thoughts were elsewhere.

Phillip knew he'd been fortunate in life but one never knew when despair and ruin might come knocking at the door. It did well to be kind and to do to others as you'd have them do to you. Hailing from humble beginnings themselves, his parents had always taught him that.

Phillip turned a corner and found himself in Upper Wimpole Street. It was clearly a genteel locality with an air of middle-class prosperity about it.

Ash trees lined the pavement and the tall town houses had clean and white exteriors. Phillip couldn't help but note, however, that there wasn't quite the level of wealth here as there was in Kensington Church Street.

It made him feel a little more confident about the call. It was unlikely his 'new money' would be met with disdain here.

In a couple more strides, he was standing outside the Banister residence. The small front garden was carpeted in baby blue crocuses and an ivy plant crept up the wall next to the freshly painted red front door. He took one more deep breath, straightened his top hat and raised his hand to the polished brass door knocker.

A Gentleman Caller

'A diplomat!' Mrs Banister's usually stony persona had evaporated and the unfortunate events of the previous day were forgiven. Her face was flushed with colour and animated with excitement. Phillip had just taken his leave and she could finally remove her mask and relax.

'It is indeed wonderful and exciting news!' Mr Banister added, nodding his head with pride. Lily was in a spin of delight as she leaped round the house in a frenzy.

'And his father is William Montgomery too!' She laughed. 'The William Montgomery of Montgomery's store! Just think of all those dresses, ribbons, hats and lady's perfumes. I'll be in heaven!'

Rose smiled and made an effort to savour the moment whilst Nell fussed with the flowers and then went to find them some water.

It was unusual for such spirits to seize the whole household and, though Rose felt a pang of something that felt curiously bitter-sweet, she did her best to brush it away.

She couldn't remember a time she'd seen her parents look so happy. If only the jubilation could be bottled up for ever.

She wished they could hire a photographer to capture the joyful mood though naturally such short notice would never do and her parents would disapprove of the cost.

Phillip had been just as presentable as the previous day in his elegant lounging jacket and well-tailored shirt, waistcoat and trousers.

Nell had instantly ushered him inside and taken his hat. He'd then stood in the sitting-room, waiting for the Banisters who all tried their hardest to be calm and composed, as if such visits took place every day.

Rose knew that her parents were becoming increasingly concerned about the prospects of their daughters and their place in society.

Lily's beauty had not gone unnoticed and she had had several callers in the last eighteen months or so but so far none of them had met with the Banisters' approval. They were social climbers and these were insecure times.

It wasn't a subject that Mrs Banister liked to talk about much, but her mother had been a seamstress, and losing her husband, who had been a tailor, tragically early in their marriage, she had toiled long and hard to keep her family afloat.

Rose also knew that the marriage to her father, a banker in the City and a hard-working and quiet gentleman, had been a fortunate match for her mother.

Neither her father nor mother had much experience of society and securing good matches for their daughters remained something of a stormy cloud lurking on the horizon. It grew larger, darker and more threatening with each year that passed by and Rose knew her days with her family were numbered.

She thought back to the visit that morning.

'I've come to enquire after Miss Lily,' Phillip had said warmly, though Rose could tell he was a little nervous as his voice was fairly fast and his eloquently pronounced syllables were slightly high pitched.

'Oh, I have made a full recovery,' Lily had assured him in return, with a quick glance in her sister's direction. Neither of them met their mother's eye.

'Splendid,' Phillip replied. Lily beamed and Rose could see the young man was both dazzled and charmed by her sister's smile. She never missed an opportunity to light up a room. There was a pause where no-one was quite sure what to say.

'What beautiful flowers,' Rose ventured. Phillip seemed to have temporarily forgotten all about them.

'Oh, yes.' He gave a little jolt and,

somewhat awkwardly, held them out. Taking the hint, Lily quickly moved over to claim them and they all marvelled at the brilliant yellow of the daffodils combined with the gentle dusty pinks of the peonies and tulips.

Rose glanced out of the window as her mother invited Phillip to sit down and Nell was sent to fetch morning tea. The spring bulbs in the Banisters' modest but tidy back garden were shooting up all over the place, replacing the greyness of winter with bright bursts of colour.

Her parents had always loved nature which was why they had picked flower names for both their daughters.

They talked for around half an hour. Phillip told them all about his role at the British Embassy and of his office on the fifth floor of the building which overlooked the impressive Arc de Triomphe, which commemorated all those lost in the French Revolutionary and Napoleonic Wars.

'It doesn't seem so very long ago that

they built it,' Mr Banister reflected as he sipped his tea, 'although I suppose it's thirty years now. I'm just thankful we are at peace with the French, for now at least.'

'Oh, Papa, enough of history and politics!' Lily interjected with an impatient laugh. 'I want to hear all about Paris! The fashions, the people, the sights!'

'Lily, please!' Mrs Banister cried, looking mortified, but their visitor was gazing at her as if he had lost himself entirely and was clearly still under her spell, though once Phillip started talking about the Champs Elysée, the Louvre Gallery and the newly restored mediaeval cathedral, Notre Dame, it was the Banister family's turn for enchantment.

He told them how the sweet scents of chocolate, cinnamon and freshly baked croissants would fill the streets as glamorous ladies dressed in the fashionable bright colours Lily had mentioned only the previous day, swanned by.

This time, Mrs Banister didn't complain of their garishness and continued to listen in a daze of wonder.

He spoke of a hill named Montmartre which had only recently become part of the city. There were several windmills at the top and the area was quickly becoming popular with artists and musicians.

'I often take a Sunday afternoon stroll up there,' Phillip said. 'The view of the city is quite spectacular from the top, especially on a clear day.'

'How marvellous,' Mr Banister replied and his wife nodded vigorously.

Rose looked away, unable to suppress a wry smile. In London, both her parents steered clear of the theatre district on a matter of principle and were rather dismissive of anything 'artistic'. In Paris, however, clearly different rules would apply.

The visit wore on. Nell supplied them with more tea and, on Mrs Banister's instructions some toasted teacakes which were usually reserved for Sundays.

Phillip spoke of his father's store which was met by a lot of excitement from Lily who asked more questions about the new season's fashions than their guest was able to answer.

After a while Mr Banister gently interjected by enquiring about the day-to-day business of the embassy and though Phillip explained that much of it was fairly mundane, especially at his level, they did, when working on top sensitive issues, pass messages to London in invisible ink.

'It was always a schoolboy dream of mine.' Their visitor laughed and seemed to have finally relaxed.

Rose noticed how he sat more comfortably in his chair now and his voice was slower and deeper than before.

'How wonderful,' she said. The rest of her family looked up at the sound of Rose's voice. It was almost as if they'd forgotten she was there. 'It's like something C. Auguste Dupin might use when solving a particularly cryptic mystery.'

'Oh, Rose, who on earth is Mr Dupin?' Lily replied rolling her eyes. 'He can't be anyone of our acquaintance.'

'Actually, he's a fictional character invented by the writer Edgar Allan Poe,' Phillip explained. 'A favourite of mine, in fact.' He caught Rose's eye and she found herself smiling into his thoughtful brown eyes.

She fought the urge to ask him which of Poe's works he liked best and if he'd read 'The Raven', one of her personal favourites.

After all, this visit was all about Lily. He'd bought flowers especially for her, and anyway, her mother wouldn't have liked of her talking about reading in the presence of important company like this. She already disapproved of the amount of time Rose spent with her books.

'You'll never be as pretty as Lily, but you risk losing the looks you do have, Rose,' she had said once, when Rose was caught up in a particularly exciting novel which she couldn't put down. 'You spend so much time indoors reading that your skin will pale even more and your eyes will all but close up if you insist on staying up late with nothing to see by but candlelight.'

Phillip was talking again and Rose did her best to shake off these thoughts and listen.

'There's quite a to-do at the moment,' he was saying, 'about the new Paris Exhibition.'

'Oh that sounds exciting,' Lily said, tilting her head to one side. Her golden ringlets bobbed gently against the mauve coloured sleeve of her day dress. Rose knew her sister would be glad she'd chosen such a fashionable garment.

Mauve may not have been the boldest and most vibrant colour available but it was new to the market as the dye hadn't long been invented, and Rose knew how proud Lily was to possess such a current piece.

'It is,' Phillip agreed, draining the last

of his second cup of tea. 'After the success of the World Fair two years ago, this new event was proposed to celebrate its success. It's also to mark the culmination of the French Empire.'

'How interesting,' Lily murmured. Rose tried to suppress another wry smile. Lily was clearly trying her best to appear well informed.

'There will be over fifty thousand exhibits,' Phillip went on. 'There will be the latest inventions, paintings, statues, as well as a wealth of international food.'

'Simply splendid,' Mrs Banister breathed.

This time Rose made an excuse and temporarily left the room for a private giggle and shake of her head. Her mother had never tried a foreign dish in her life.

In fact Rose had recently bought some Welsh cakes home from a bakery on Oxford Street and even those had been met with a great sense of suspicion.

She returned to the sitting-room to hear their visitor speaking of his plans to return to Paris with his mother for the start of the exhibition in a few weeks' time and then escort her to the city of Nice. It would seem that the visit had come to a close as he was standing up now and Nell was sent to find him his hat.

'I shall call again, if I may?' he asked as the Banister family joined him in the hallway. It was just a little too narrow to comfortably fit five adults and despite the chilly weather outdoors, Rose suddenly felt stiflingly hot.

'We would be honoured,' Mr Banister replied solemnly as he took their guest's hand. And with that, the gentleman caller was gone, pausing only to raise a hand at the front gate as Lily sidled past her parents to position herself right at the front door. She proceeded to wave joyfully to him as he bid the family farewell.

A Stab of Envy

'Oh, Rose, can you believe it?' Dusk had fallen and the sisters had retired to Lily's bedroom to talk about the events of the day.

Lily had brought the flowers upstairs when their mother wasn't looking and had placed them on her dressing table. She lounged on the bed in her nightdress whilst Rose sat back in the armchair and looked out of the window.

For some reason the sight of the bouquet triggered a melancholy feeling within her and it helped to look away.

The sun had set and the sky was darkening though a thin band of sky in the west had resisted the inevitable and remained a deep shade of royal blue.

'Actually, I can,' Rose turned from the window and smiled at her sister. 'And thank goodness your caller is suitable this time.'

'He's more than suitable — he's a diplomat!' Lily almost shrieked the last word.

'I can't wait to write and tell Julia. Just imagine how jealous she'll be.'

'Lily,' Rose said in a low and cautionary tone, 'it's not becoming to be smug and anyway, let's not get carried away just yet. It's just the one visit, after all.'

Later, after Lily had finally tired herself out from all her chatter and Rose had retreated to her own room to sleep, she found she was unable to settle down to rest.

She sat up in bed, lit a candle and tried to read, but found she couldn't concentrate on her book, either. Lily's remark about Julia had triggered her thoughts back to her plans for the future and now they consumed her entirely.

Julia Marchmont was a friend from their childhood. Their fathers worked together at the bank and their mothers were friends too. Julia was a couple of years older than Rose, and had generally played a bossy 'older sister' role in their lives.

The fact that Julia's father was senior to Mr Banister at the bank increased her sense of authority over the Banister girls.

Her house, a few streets away, was bigger than theirs with a larger back garden, too. Her mother had three maids and a cook and Julia always had more dresses, shoes, ribbons and hats than the Banister sisters.

'Mama bought me this new evening dress for our trip to the Royal Opera House,' she would say as she twirled around in her new garment.

'Julia is a big show-off,' Lily had pouted on more than one occasion. 'She's not as special as she thinks she is. Plus everyone knows that money can't buy a beautiful face!'

'Lily, don't!' Rose had said. 'It's not ladylike to make such catty remarks. And anyway, it's not Julia's fault that her father earns more money than ours.

We're more fortunate than many, just remember that.'

Unlike her sister, Rose kept her pangs of jealousy at bay, and genuinely got on well with Julia. Perhaps it was because they were closer in age and were both interested in novels, languages and music, that they became firm friends.

Rose would let Julia take centre stage and would enjoy hearing about dances, operas, ballets and afternoon teas, without harbouring a deep-seated resentment, like Lily. Deep down she suspected Julia was jealous, not only of Lily's good looks but of their relationship as sisters, too, as she was an only child.

Rose did her best to see past the material wealth and the occasional patronising remark and met their friend with kindness, as she would wish others would do to her.

Julia had met her husband, a wealthy viscount named Bartholomew Laidlaw, during her first season on the London social circuit several years ago now and moved to his coastal residence in Brighton not long after their wedding.

Rose continued to exchange letters with her and knew that their oldest child was nearing five and would soon be in need of a governess. Soon, very soon now, she would write to Julia to offer her services.

After all, Brighton wasn't so very far away, especially now the railroads made travel so much easier. She could visit her family during any time off and most importantly she'd be amongst friends.

She knew Lily and most probably their mother would baulk at the idea of her becoming part of Julia's staff, but she had to think strategically and surely this would be the lesser of two evils.

★　★　★

The knock at the door at almost precisely the same time as the previous day took all the Banister family by surprise.

45

'I do beg your pardon for calling again so soon,' Phillip had said as he stood in the hallway. 'I won't stay long.'

He had removed his hat and clutched it in his hands. Rose noticed that his knuckles were white and his face was flushed. His voice was slightly high pitched again, too.

'I would like, if I may, to invite Miss Lily to accompany my mother and me to France,' he went on hurriedly, 'to the exhibition and to the French Rivera thereafter. My mother will be with us at all times and there is ample space in the accommodation for us all — if she would like to join us, that is.'

His face flushed deeper as he made some more remarks about the trip to fill the stunned silence that consumed the room.

Rose glanced at her parents who could barely conceal their excitement and then at Lily who was beaming from ear to ear.

Rose smiled too as the chorus of acceptance began. She heard herself say, 'How wonderful,' 'How splendid,' and 'What joy!' but a nagging sense of something she couldn't quite identify pulled tightly at her soul.

It pinched, stung and slapped, until her inner self, the part of her she kept hidden away and barely acknowledged herself, couldn't help but succumb to the cold stab of envy and despair.

Travel Plans

Phillip left the Banisters' house and made his way back down Upper Wimpole Street in a daze of incredulity and excitement.

The weather had changed again and the day had turned out very sunny, but Phillip was barely aware of his surroundings at all and almost walked into a street vendor's sweetmeats stall when he went to cross over the road.

'Sorry, good sir, my mind is elsewhere,' he explained when the vendor gave a 'Tut' of disapproval and annoyance.

Phillip would have happily told him all about his wonderful news, had the man looked a little less grumpy, but took the hint and continued on his way.

It felt later in the year than March. The sun was high in an endlessly blue sky and the spring breeze felt warm against his face.

The sense of relief was immense. He had walked to the Banisters' that morning in a buzz of adrenaline and nerves with his mood dipping and diving like a migrating swallow in a midsummer sky.

He couldn't shake off the feeling that inviting Lily to join them might be something of a mistake. Would the Banisters find the suggestion improper, he worried as he glanced into a milliner's window and instantly found himself imagining Lily in one of the elegant hats on display.

It was as if her face was etched all over him in that invisible ink he had talked of in their sitting-room the previous day. He could hear the joyous notes of her laugh reverberating through his ears at all hours of the day and he was acutely aware of them when he settled down to sleep.

It felt as if a rare malady had infected him in both body and soul and he wasn't even sure of himself any more.

The trip to France which had previously held such pleasant prospects now loomed on the horizon like a spectacular but dangerous storm.

Phillip knew he would never forgive himself if he embarked on the journey without Lily, yet the prospect of asking her terrified him.

'Of course you must invite Miss Lily,' his mother had reassured him, when he returned home the previous day and opened up about his call that morning.

He had remembered to purchase a bouquet of daffodils from that same flower seller in Marble Arch.

Sally, their maid, had instantly placed them in water right by his mother's chaise longue which overlooked their landscaped back garden, which was blossoming into a myriad of colours, thanks to the numerous spring bulbs their gardener had planted in the autumn.

Mrs Montgomery lay on the chaise longue now and although that persistent chest cough from her recent viral infection still wasn't showing any signs of disappearing, Phillip's news had brought a spark to her eyes and she couldn't stop smiling at him.

'You really don't mind, Mama?' he had asked. Their plan had been to spend some special time together with a series of gentle pursuits suited to the fragility of her health.

The trip to the French Rivera would be a change of scene for them both and he had hoped to unwind in the beauty of the coast there too.

The addition of Lily to the party would change the dynamic entirely. His mother would go from companion to chaperone and any sense of relaxation would be lost with a young lady to impress and entertain.

'This is a marvellous opportunity, Phillip,' Mrs Montgomery replied. 'We can easily book a third ticket on the steamship and you have no idea how long I've hoped and prayed that such a great thing would happen to you.'

She was so animated that some of her words were lost in a fit of coughs, but she continued nevertheless.

'We haven't pushed you, your father and I, as we married for love and would wish the same for you. But lately I've been worrying that perhaps we should have given you a little more guidance in such matters, as, after all, you really are such a quiet young man. But once again, you have proven you have your own mind and Miss Lily sounds like an excellent choice. I haven't felt so excited for years.'

Phillip smiled and felt a lump form in his throat. He had never realised how much his parents wanted a happy match for him.

He hadn't been sure what his father would think about his proposal to invite Lily on their trip either.

Phillip Senior was so absorbed by the store that it was hard sometimes to coax him into any kind of conversation beyond the weather or what Cook might be preparing for dinner.

He knew how strongly Phillip approved of the trip to France as he often felt guilty that his wife spent so much time alone. Phillip had worried that his father would disapprove about the change in dynamic but from his mother's reaction, it would appear that such fears weren't necessary.

'So, do tell me all about her,' Mrs Montgomery prompted as she sat back in her chair and closed her eyes. 'I want to know absolutely everything, from the very beginning.'

Obliging, Phillip told his mother all about Lily's fall at Hyde Park and they laughed together about the absurdity of it all.

'I have a feeling it was all my fault anyway,' Phillip said. 'I was so caught up in my thoughts about the embassy, I stood right in front of them and I think she was jumping up to get a better view.'

'Oh goodness, my love,' his mother chuckled. She had sat up now and was wiping at her eyes with one of her delicate lace handkerchiefs. 'Only you could cause a refined young lady to fall in the mud and then strike up a courtship! I'm surprised she let you through the front door.'

'I did wonder,' Phillip admitted, laughing too. 'Miss Lily certainly made a hasty retreat from the park without staying long to make my acquaintance. Her sister spoke for her, in fact. Thankfully all is forgiven now.'

'It sounds like you may have found a kindred spirit, Phillip,' his mother remarked as she lay back again. 'You're not so comfortable in company either.'

'Well, I thought that, too,' Phillip replied. 'But now that I've called on her and the family, I can see that she is actually very talkative and at times pretty forthright. It was simply the shock of the fall that made her so meek.'

'I suppose that's natural. She would have been quite mortified, I'm sure. So, tell me about her interests. Is she a bookworm like you? Does she speak languages, play a musical instrument, or like history?'

'I must confess, I'm not sure,' Phillip said. He didn't want to tell his mother quite how stunned he was by her beauty and how he struggled to remember anything else about her. There were some matters which weren't for sharing with one's parents. 'She was excited by my stories of Paris and most of her questions were about ladies' fashions, on which I'm hardly an expert.'

'No.' His mother laughed. Phillip went on to talk about the Banisters' charming town-house on Upper Wimpole Street, with the spring flowers blooming all over the back garden and ivy creeping up the front wall.

He told her of Mr Banister's role at the bank and how much Lily had loved the bouquet of flowers he'd bought for the household, but had very definitely claimed for herself.

On reflection, he should have bought a bunch for her sister as well.

'Miss Rose likes reading Poe too,' he mentioned when Mrs Banister had asked about more Lily's sister. 'She is quite reserved but really came alive when she talked of his work. The rest of the family were keen to carry on talking about Paris though, so I didn't get much chance to speak to her further.'

Something told Phillip that he would have quite a lot in common with Rose, more so than with Lily, if truth were told. As he talked, his thoughts kept straying back to the way her face had lit up at the mention of Poe but for some reason, he didn't say any more to his mother about her and all his instincts told him to push any thoughts of her from his mind.

He focused instead on Miss Lily's bewitching smile and the charming chime of her laugh as it rang out around the Banisters' sitting-room. By the time Phillip paused for breath and looked at his mother for a response, he realised she'd fallen into a deep and contented sleep.

Unexpected Setback

Phillip burst through the front door of his family's home at Kensington Church Street triumphant with joy and itching to break the happy news to his mother.

He was also planning to tell the cook, the maids, the gardener, his mother's best friend and anyone else who happened to come by the house between now and their departure to Paris.

As soon as Phillip walked through the door, however, he was met by the imposing figure of William Montgomery and his jubilation faded into the light spring breeze. It was unusual for his father to be home in the middle of a working day.

Phillip had been looking forward to telling his father the news but wasn't banking on breaking it to him quite so soon. One look at his father's grave face, however, told him that today was not to be a day of good tidings.

His stomach dipped in panic and despair as he struggled to form the correct words.

'It's Mama, isn't it?' He had known she wasn't herself, but his preoccupation with Lily had absorbed him so utterly that somehow he had pushed his worries for his mother to one side.

Guilt surged through him for the second time that week and he cursed himself for being so blinded by his own pursuit of happiness.

'She's not at all well, Phillip,' his father replied. 'Sally rushed over to the store herself to find me and then to call on the doctor, whilst Cook sat with your mother at home. Dr Price is upstairs now and thinks she has pneumonia.'

'Oh, goodness,' Phillip followed his father into the sitting-room and sank into one of the easy chairs.

His stomach still churned and he

placed his hands to his head. The sun beamed through the windows but he suddenly felt unnaturally cold as a chill took over his whole body.

'When she awoke from a mid-morning sleep, she could hardly breathe,' Phillip's father explained. 'Her cough has become increasingly worse and she has excruciating pain in her chest and shoulders. Then Sally noticed that her face was looking swollen as well. That's when she came to find me and Dr Price was called.'

Phillip's own breathing felt laboured as he tried to take in the news. Ailments, infections and maladies were everywhere one looked, yet somehow he hadn't seriously considered that any would come knocking at his own front door.

They were fortunate people, the Montgomerys, and could afford to take necessary precautions. They had modern conveniences like clean running water in the house and stayed away from dangerous places such as the East End where infections like typhoid, cholera and consumption could be found lurking at every street corner.

Still, he shouldn't have been so naïve to think they were safe from every peril of ill health, he thought as a fresh wave of guilt swept him away. He only half listened as his father told him that the disease had probably come as a result of her viral infection.

'Do they think . . . ?' Phillip stopped, unable to finish his sentence.

'We don't know,' his father answered abruptly but then, as Phillip felt his face begin to crumple, Phillip's voice softened. 'Dr Price has prescribed a wealth of medicine,' he said. 'Our bedroom looks like an alchemist's shop.

'He thinks that providing she responds well to the treatment and with the right level of rest, she may just pull through, but I won't believe that till she's laughing and out lunching with the ladies again.'

'Can I see her?' Phillip asked.

'Yes, she's been asking for you and Dr Price has advised that she's past the infectious stage now.'

Phillip rushed up the stairs and was by his mother's bedside in an instant. She was propped up on several pillows and wearing a great many layers of warm clothes with a nightcap on her head.

'I'm so sorry,' she whispered as he took her hand. It felt worryingly thin as well as being damp and cool.

'It's me who should apologise, Mama,' Phillip replied, feeling his eyes fill with tears. 'I can't believe I've been so selfish. I should have noticed you were becoming unwell.'

'Your mind has been elsewhere, Phillip,' his mother replied. Her face was wan and swollen but the beginning of a smile was flickering on her pale lips. 'It's natural and I'm so happy you're finally courting,' she went on.

'I'll tell Miss Lily the trip's postponed,' Phillip answered. 'We'll go when you're fit and well. Not a second before.'

'Absolutely not,' Mrs Montgomery replied. Her voice was hoarse but Phillip heard a steely determination in it too. 'As I just said, I'm sorry not to be joining you but the tickets and accommodation are booked and I won't let you miss the exhibition for a second time. I won't let you postpone this trip, Phillip. I insist.'

'But how will we . . . ?' Phillip began.

'You'll think of something,' his mother replied, closing her eyes once more.

Antics on Oxford Street

'Bonjour,' Lily practised whilst twirling around in one of her newly purchased dresses and admiring herself in her bedroom mirror.

Mrs Banister had given in to Lily's requests for new garments, in the light of the new and exciting circumstances, and she had a whole new wardrobe dedicated to the year of pizazz after all.

She was currently in a tightly fitting magenta evening dress with very narrow skirts. It showed off her petite frame.

'You'll need to learn more than just 'Bonjour', Lily,' Rose remarked, who was, once again, sitting in the armchair by the window.

Lily had hardly retained any of the French they had learned together with Miss Pritchard and really just knew greetings and the odd random phrase.

'Oh, Phillip speaks French so it'll be fine,' Lily said as she began rooting around in one of the cupboards. 'I don't think I have a hat to match this dress,' she went on.

'Remember that he's Mr Montgomery to you until you're engaged, Lily,' Rose reminded her sternly. 'It would be most presumptive and rude to use his given name before you're invited to do so.'

'Oh, it just sounds so stuffy,' Lily replied, pouting. 'I promise I'll remember when I see him, but there's no harm in referring to him as Phillip when it's just the two of us.'

Rose sighed. She didn't have the spirit to reason further with her younger sister.

'Now,' Lily continued, 'I have a problem. I simply don't have a suitable hat to go with this dress. Do come to town with me, Rose, to try to find something pretty.'

Rose rolled her eyes but began preparations for going into town. She didn't relish trailing after Lily round the shops, but the house was beginning to feel uncomfortably warm and she welcomed the chance to get outdoors, especially as it looked to be another pleasant day.

★ ★ ★

Clearly most of Marylebone had had the same idea as the omnibus was crowded and, like the Banisters' townhouse, too hot. The straw which covered the floor gave off a strong smell and the stuffy air was thick with snuff.

Rose couldn't help but wonder if this had been such a good idea after all. A parasol belonging to the lady behind her was digging uncomfortably into her back and the discomfort worsened with every jolt of the carriage.

She looked out of the window to distract herself with London life outside. There were the usual street vendors, servants on errands, men sitting high as they rode the new Penny

Farthing bicycle and elegant folk gliding by in a luxurious bubble of sophistication and privilege.

Lily was right about bright colours being in fashion. They were like a vibrant rainbow splashed across the grey of the London streets.

Rose turned her head after the omnibus had trundled further along. They were on Oxford Street now. She could still see the sunshine yellow gown that one of the fancy women was wearing. It was like a summer sunbeam flickering amidst the clouds in a dull iron sky.

Lily, of course, hadn't stopped chatting since they left Upper Wimpole Street, but Rose found she had all but detached herself from the monologue and could only hope she was nodding and murmuring agreement in the right places. It was a technique she'd been perfecting since childhood.

'So Montgomery's is first stop,' Lily said, in the midst of talking about the wide range of ladies' gloves which were available nowadays.

'Pardon?' Rose had jolted to attention at the mention of the name.

'We're going to the store. It'll be 'our store' soon. Oh Rose, I said that ages ago. I knew you weren't listening properly.'

'Is that a good idea? I mean, we're not acquainted with the Montgomery family yet, so it would be improper to introduce ourselves and yet it seems wrong to waltz by like strangers. Why not wait until your courtship is more established?'

'You're such a bore, Rose,' Lily replied, pouting and folding her arms, with a sigh that sounded like a 'huff'. 'Phillip Senior is the boss of the whole shop. He's hardly likely to be walking the floors.'

'I don't know. If I ran a shop, I would like to check that all was in order.'

'It's not likely that he'll be around when we're there. He'll be too busy being important somewhere else. Come on, Rose. I want to imagine what it'll feel like when I'm the daughter-in-law of the helm of the store and can have absolutely anything I want!'

'No,' Rose replied stonily. 'Come, it's our stop.' The sisters rose and weaved their way through the other passengers to alight from the coach. The incoming breeze was welcome as the door of the omnibus swung open and the sisters got off. Before Rose could stop her, Lily set off at a pace. With a dip to her insides, Rose knew what was coming.

'Lily!' she called several times but her sister only gestured for her to follow. A few people were turning to look, so Rose didn't call out again. Begrudging and irritated she kept up with the bobbing figure of her sister in front of her. She seemed to spend half her life running round London after Lily.

A Testing Experience

Rose's worst fears were confirmed when Lily's petite figure strode up to the pearly marble steps and large glass doors of Montgomery's store, and, without a moment's hesitation, hopped up and walked straight inside.

Usually Rose stopped to admire the diamond pattern on the white tiled floor, take in the attractive displays and allow the delicate floral scents of the perfumery transport her to another world.

Lavender, jasmine and honeysuckle filled the air and Rose would imagine herself in a pleasant country garden bathed in sunbeams, no matter what the weather was doing outside. Today, however, there was no time for such fancies.

'Right, Lily,' she said in her best 'no nonsense' voice. Rose had tried for some time now to emulate her mother's stern tone when Lily was in one of her particularly forthright moods but had never quite managed it, somehow. 'If you're looking for accessories, we'll need to head over there and to the left.'

'Oh, I want to have a good look round first,' Lily replied with a wicked grin. She was as breathtaking as ever with the azuline dress she was wearing highlighting the blue of her eyes, yet Rose couldn't help but notice that she didn't look at all demure today. She was a woman with shopping on her mind.

Rose watched helplessly as Lily flitted around the perfumery, like a butterfly in a wild flower meadow, lifting each and every glass bottle to inhale its scent. She insisted on dabbing a little of each one on to her handkerchiefs, gloves and even the sleeves of her dress too.

After she'd tried a dozen or so bottles, the shop assistant who had been watching her for some time decided it was time to intervene. She had been watching with curiosity at first, but Rose could tell by the slight frown that was forming on her brow, that it was quickly transforming into disapproval.

'Excuse me, miss,' she began. Rose guessed that she was about Lily's age but her voice was deep and her look rather intimidating. She seemed more mature than both of them and gave off a definite air of authority.

'Yes?' Lily shot her a disarming smile.

'We do advise customers to test just one or two scents at a time,' the young lady replied. Her face was still disapproving and she was clearly unimpressed. 'The essence of the perfumes do rather blend into one if they're all used at once.'

The magic that normally surrounded Lily appeared to have fizzled out and those two spots of colour on her cheeks that always appeared when she felt self-conscious were there again.

'Of course,' she answered meekly. It wasn't long, however, before Rose noticed her sister take one last bottle of orange blossom cologne when the stern assistant's back was turned, and, with a stubborn purse of her lips, she removed a ribbon from her dress pocket and dipped it somewhat defiantly into the scented liquid.

Rose was about to whisper a quiet reprimand but Lily was already striding away from the perfumery to peruse the rest of the store and Rose had no choice but to follow her. Lily left a botanical mist in her wake that smelled so sweet, it was dizzying.

Lily rushed around the millinery section of Montgomery's in much the same way as she had the perfumery but, if anything, drew even more attention to them by twirling around and admiring herself in everything she tried on.

'Doesn't this work perfectly, Rose?' she said as she perched a small feathery hat on her head. Her blonde ringlets followed under it as if it were made especially for her. The hat was exactly the same shade of azuline as her dress and her eyes looked bluer than ever.

The assistant in accessories was busy with another customer so Lily had a temporary free rein over the department and seemed determined to make the most of every second.

Rose stole a peep at the assistant who was nodding and bustling around for her well-dressed customer. Something about the young lady's earnest smile and wide blinking green eyes told Rose that she may not have been made of quite the same stuff as her colleague in the perfumery.

'Remember that you came to look for a purple hat to match that evening gown,' Rose reminded her sister as Lily picked up a delicate lace dress cap and examined it intently.

'It's magenta, Rose, but you're right, of course, as usual. Now, let me have a look.' The dress cap was instantly discarded as Lily scanned the shelves. 'Oh, look there!'

Rose saw where Lily was gesturing

and with a sinking heart realised what was happening. The keen young member of staff was wrapping up a vibrant, feather topped magenta cap in crisp brown paper, which would soon be placed in that well-dressed customer's shopping basket, which was already overflowing with expensive looking purchases.

'I need that one,' Lily cried, running over. The elegant lady turned to leave and Rose saw with a lurch to her stomach that it was Harriet Marchmont, their neighbour and Julia's mother. How typical that they'd see someone of their acquaintance just when Lily was about to make another spectacle of herself.

Thankfully, Mrs Marchmont had turned and was making her way towards the exit of the shop. Lily was too busy pestering the shop assistant to notice that they knew the departing customer.

'Oh, I'm terribly sorry, miss,' the shop assistant was saying. Her voice was fast and those green eyes were blinking furiously. 'I've just sold the last one. We have this lovely hat in mauve though, if you'd like to step this way?'

'Oh, please,' Lily wailed in her most beseeching voice. 'Mauve just simply won't do. Couldn't you possibly just have a little look in your storeroom? I could come with you and help . . . '

'Oh, no, we're not allowed to let anyone in there,' the young lady started to say.

'I insist,' Lily replied. 'I could find a needle in a haystack, everyone says so.'

And with that Lily made her way towards a door behind the till, which said in very large letters *Staff Only*.

'You there! Stop!' came the thunderous roar of the perfumery assistant who'd noticed Lily's antics from the other side of the store. 'That's trespassing!'

'Lily, quick,' Rose cried, running to her sister and taking her by the arm. 'I'm terribly sorry,' she said to the staff. The perfumery assistant was crimson with rage whilst the millinery assistant resembled a startled wild animal.

'What is all this?' came a voice. It was kindly but full of authority. Rose knew with one glance at his large hazel eyes and wavy dark hair that he couldn't be anyone other than Phillip Senior. The family resemblance was uncanny despite his thick beard and moustache.

'A misunderstanding, sir, we're leaving,' Rose replied quickly, as both sisters swept past him, their heads to the floor. Rose was fairly sure she heard the perfumery assistant mutter 'Good riddance' after them as they bid a hasty retreat.

The sisters were nearly at the store entrance when another loud voice stopped them in their tracks.

'Rose, Lily, how splendid to see you!' Harriet Marchmont had evidently become distracted by the perfumery counter and had yet to actually leave the shop.

Rose wasn't sure if she'd heard the

fracas from before. If Mrs Marchmont had indeed seen the trouble they'd almost got into, she was gracious enough not to mention it and appeared genuinely pleased to see them.

'Mrs Marchmont, good afternoon.' Rose felt herself smiling weakly. Lily, who had been silent since Rose had taken her by her arm, murmured a greeting too.

'I really must invite you ladies and your mother to tea sometime soon,' Mrs Marchmont went on. 'It's simply been far too long. Oh, and I have some marvellous news too. Julia is expecting her third child.'

'How lovely — congratulations!' Rose answered warmly. She had known Julia was pregnant for some time from their exchange of letters, but felt an expression of surprise was expected. 'And yes, we would be delighted, thank you, Mrs Marchmont, but pressing matters mean we must return home now.'

The perfumery assistant had now returned to her usual station, not far from where the sisters were standing and Rose could feel her angry eyes burning into them. It was more than necessary that they made an immediate exit from the store.

Rose felt every jolt of the omnibus on the way back to Marylebone. This time a gentleman's walking stick was digging into her back. She did wish that someone would invent a mode of transport which was a little more comfortable and spacious.

'Oh goodness, he saw us,' Lily lamented sitting next to her. 'Whatever will I say when we're introduced?'

'Hopefully he won't make the connection,' Rose said soothingly in reply. 'It was all so fleeting that he probably won't remember.'

'I hope so,' Lily replied, still crestfallen. 'And I didn't even get to buy that beautiful azuline hat. When I'm the new Mrs Montgomery, I'll be giving that perfumery busybody a piece of my mind and preferably her marching orders.'

'You'll be living in Paris, remember,' Rose answered, staring out of the window. The pleasant day had transitioned into a dull one and it was beginning to spit with rain.

'Oh, yes,' Lily replied dreamily. 'Such a shame there wasn't time for me to tell Mrs Marchmont about my forthcoming trip.

'I'd have loved to see her face. It would have put a stop to her boasting about her third grandchild, that's for sure. What was she doing buying that magenta hat anyway? It's far too young for her.'

'I expect it was for Julia.'

'Typical,' Lily muttered. 'Even now that she lives in Brighton that wretched girl still gets whatever it is I want. You wait till I'm a diplomat's wife, Julia Marchmont. Just you wait.'

* * *

The sisters were weary, damp and ready for a cup of tea when they arrived home at Upper Wimpole Street. The rain was coming down fast now. As soon as they entered the house, Rose knew something was amiss. Her parents were in the sitting-room with their heads close together and Nell was scuttling around in the kitchen and vigorously cleaning the work surfaces, despite them already being spotless.

'Not a word, Rose,' Lily whispered unnecessarily to her sister as they tidied themselves in the hallway. Both the Banister girls knew how their mother would react if she heard of today's escapade. Thankfully there wasn't any evidence this time.

'Ah, you're back. Good.' Mr Banister had emerged from the sitting-room. His face was very solemn.

'Whatever is the matter, Papa?' Lily asked. Her face had paled and Rose felt herself shudder with fear. She had a feeling that whatever it was, it had something to do with the trip to Paris. The store staff couldn't possibly have known who they were and sent word to

Phillip Junior to cancel Lily's involvement in the trip. There wouldn't be time, even by electric telegraph. Or would there?

'Phillip called by when you two were out,' Mrs Banister said when the sisters were sitting down. 'Unfortunately his mother has fallen ill with pneumonia and won't be able to travel for some time.'

'How horrible,' Rose said, her relief replaced by concern. 'So is the trip postponed?'

'Well, he doesn't want to do that,' Mrs Banister coloured slightly as she spoke. 'He's actually invited me too, as a chaperone.'

'You!' Lily let out a snort of derision and Rose could barely conceal a smile. The idea was utterly preposterous. Elizabeth Banister had never even boarded a steam train.

'I'm glad to have provided you two with so much amusement,' Mrs Banister said, the angry vein throbbed in her temple again and she looked rather hurt. 'I can barely believe I raised two daughters with such little respect for their elders.'

'Sorry, Mama,' the sisters replied in unison.

'Still, clearly I can't possibly go,' Mrs Banister went on. 'I don't care for travelling and, unlike you, I didn't have the privilege of a proper education growing up, so am unable to speak French either. Though I must say that given the antics of the pair of you in recent times, I'm not sure Miss Pritchard was worth the money.'

Rose felt her face flush, despite knowing that her mother's remark wasn't entirely fair.

'So I can't go?' Lily was close to tears.

'Well, that all depends,' Mrs Banister was staring at Rose with steely and unblinking eyes. 'Your father and I put over a counter suggestion that Mr Montgomery has accepted and we hope you do, too. As Rose speaks fluent French, is older by a couple of years and is, of the two you, slightly more sensible, we propose that she attends too, as the chaperone.'

Lily's eyes opened wide as she squeezed her sister's hand, whilst Rose found herself unable to speak. Instead, she glanced out of the window as she composed her face for a reply. The rain had finally stopped now and a blackbird swooped in the sky. From behind the slate grey and imposing dark clouds, a tiny ray of sunlight had finally peeped through.

All Aboard

Phillip felt the sea breeze against his face as they boarded the steamship at Dover. It felt good to be en route back to France. London would always be his home, but Paris was where he belonged, for now at any rate.

'The *Marie Augustine*,' Rose read out loud as they were ushered into the first class saloon. 'What a beautiful name for a ship.'

'Do hurry up,' Lily squealed. She had rushed on ahead. 'This is wonderful.' Phillip smiled fondly as Lily danced around the saloon taking in the velvet seating, polished wood floor and colourful art work of pleasant maritime scenes adorning the walls.

Then, when they heard the screech of the captain's whistle, the three of them went out on deck to watch the *Marie Augustine* set sail.

Phillip had travelled to and from France on several occasions now but seeing the excitement of the sisters allowed him to appreciate the experience through new eyes.

The vast passenger ship with its two large funnels was certainly impressive, as were the Dover docks. It wasn't long before they felt the ship's engine start up and the boat begin to move as it made its way out towards the open sea.

'Goodbye, goodbye,' Lily cried to no-one in particular as she waved her lacy handkerchief at the crowd of people who had turned up to watch.

'Look,' Phillip said to the sisters after a short time had passed, 'there are the white cliffs of Dover.'

'Goodness,' Rose breathed as the mountainous alabaster formations came into view, 'they're stunning.'

'They look as if they're smothered in snow,' Lily replied, still for once. 'They could be icebergs.'

'I'm very glad they're not.' Phillip laughed, gazing thankfully at the clear sky, dotted with only a very few small white clouds and the bright sun overhead.

March had turned into May and he was hoping for some enjoyable weather over their time in France.

He left the sisters talking to each other as they watched the sea from the deck and sat down on one of the benches to take a moment for himself.

It had seemed natural to invite Lily's mother on the trip in place of his own, plus she'd been so enthusiastic about France when he had first met the Banisters on that sunny March morning a couple of months ago.

So it came as quite a surprise that, when he made the suggestion, a look of deep shock passed over her face. Anyone would have thought he'd invited her on a voyage round uncharted seas in search of the New World.

'Well, I,' she had started, then paused. Her face looked pained and panicked. The whole thing was quite uncomfortable. It was Mr Banister who had intervened in the end and said that Lily's older sister, Rose, would make a far more suitable travel companion and he was sure she would be delighted at the opportunity to broaden her horizons.

This time it had been Phillip's turn to stall. He felt something flutter in his chest and for a moment he was disorientated. Of course the suggestion made sense, especially when the Banisters explained that she spoke fluent French too, yet somehow the idea simply hadn't occurred to him before and, if he was honest with himself, made him feel just a little uneasy.

It wasn't something he could explain, even to himself, so he had no option but to accept their proposal, on the understanding that Rose would agree, which both the Banisters very confidently assured him she would.

'Oh, what a marvellous idea!' his mother had exclaimed when he told her about the new plan for Rose to go in her place. Mrs Montgomery's cheeks were thin and her skin sallow, yet the good news had clearly perked her up and though there were grey circles around her eyes, they glowed with enthusiasm.

'Will you still take Sally to help them?' It had been in their original plan for Sally to join them on the trip too, to attend to Mrs Montgomery.

'I think you need her more than we do, Mama,' Phillip replied. He knew Sally would be disappointed to miss out on travelling to France but she and his mother were close and he was certain she'd want to stay and care for her. 'Plus the Misses Banister haven't been brought up with a lady's maid. There only seems to be one member of staff in their whole household, so I daresay they'll manage whilst we're away.'

* * *

Phillip looked at Rose as she laughed with Lily on the deck and pointed something out on the ship. The breeze had blown a little of her hair out of its somewhat severe bun and it curled in tendrils around her face which was rosier than normal and animated by the new experience.

She may not have been whooping like her younger sister but her eyes still danced with joy. They were an emerald sea green — he'd never noticed that before.

Phillip felt almost ashamed that he'd ever questioned the idea of her joining them. Her gentle personality and intelligent reasoning were the perfect balance to Lily's constant elation and endless chatter. Phillip didn't think she'd stopped for air during the whole train journey from London to Dover that morning.

It had been Rose who had quietly encouraged her to calm down and take some deep breaths so she didn't risk over-exerting herself and feeling ill.

Lily had rolled her eyes and laughed in response, but Phillip could tell by the way the sisters looked at each other sometimes and how they'd confer together with their heads almost touching that there was a real love and a close bond between them.

Already it seemed impossible and altogether wrong, somehow, that they could ever have planned to leave Rose behind.

After a little longer out on deck, the first class passengers were called to luncheon in the saloon, so Phillip and his companions made their way indoors. He enjoyed watching the sisters exclaim at the opulence and luxury of the dining-room. Again, it made a fairly regular experience for him all the more special.

'Oh, I'm far too excited to eat,' Lily announced. 'And the ship does rock so.' She looked around as the other passengers took their seats too. 'I do love the ribbons in that lady's cap,' she went on. 'I can barely wait to see the shops in Paris. Goodness, look at this bread. It's so crusty. Perhaps I am quite hungry after all.'

Phillip and Rose exchanged a smile as Lily enthusiastically buttered her slice of baguette, took a big bite and declared it delicious.

A waiter came by with French onion soup, which Lily said was beautiful, too, and for a restful few minutes was so absorbed by eating that all conversation went on hold.

'More soup, mademoiselle?' the waiter asked Lily in French. She was first to clear her bowl.

'Ah, *oui, un petit pois, si vous plait,*' Lily answered, beaming. Rose shook her head and looked away to conceal her mirth whilst the waiter smiled indulgently and ladled some more into her bowl.

'You just asked for a little pea!' Rose said, after he'd gone. She'd given way to her giggles now, though Phillip could tell that her laughter was gentle and good-natured by the way she looked at her sister, once she'd dried her eyes. 'It's *peu* you should say, not *pois.*'

'Well, *pardonnez-moi* for trying,' Lily retorted, looking at Phillip and scrunching up her nose. He knew she was seeking support so made sure his face appeared sympathetic and impartial but inside he was chuckling away to himself, too.

The waiter returned with white fish cooked in garlic and herbs with roasted potatoes and finely chopped vegetables. There was more bread placed on the table.

Realising he was peckish, Phillip tucked in and let himself enjoy the tasty flavours of French cuisine, which he had to admit, he had rather missed since being at home.

Rose seemed hungry, too. Phillip noticed that she took three slices of baguette and accepted an extra portion of potatoes when the waiter came back to the table.

'Rose, really,' he heard Lily whisper to her sister, 'we're in company.' Rose turned a little pink, but ignored her sister and began wrapping up a slice of bread and several potatoes in three separate little parcels, using some cotton handkerchiefs she'd produced from one of her pockets.

'I can't help it,' Rose replied. She smiled apologetically at Phillip. 'There's far too much food here for all of us and it just seems so wrong when there's people going without all around us.'

'Oh Rose, we're not in London any more,' Lily replied rolling her eyes.

'Don't tell me there aren't starving people in Paris, too,' Rose answered. 'And I'm pretty sure the third-class passengers weren't served a three-course luncheon like us. I shall give these food parcels to them if all else fails. How do you find Paris, Phillip, in terms of how poorer people live?'

'Well, France likes to think itself the world leader in 'liberty, equality and fraternity',' Phillip replied. 'But the reality is that Paris is as divided as London in terms of how the rich and poor live.'

'Gosh, I'm stuffed,' Lily cut in,

covering her mouth with a tiny yawn. 'I could fall asleep.'

'I regularly see chiffoniers picking through the rubbish thrown out by householders on my way to the embassy most mornings,' Phillip went on.

Rose nodded in response and Phillip could almost see the thoughts whizzing around behind her slight frown, whilst Lily gazed admiringly at a lady in a mauve morning dress holding a tiny snow-white poodle on her lap. Lily clearly wasn't following the conversation.

'Oh, sorry,' he started, realising Rose might not know the translation of this French word. 'Chiffoniers means . . . '

'Rag-pickers,' Rose interjected, 'I think?'

'Yes,' Phillip replied, impressed. 'They sort through all the waste people dump on the streets looking for items of value they can sell on,' he explained.

'Corks and glass bottles, for example, can be sold to wine merchants, bones are collected to offer toy makers for dominoes and buttons can be of interest to haberdashers and tailors.

'Did you know that stale bread can be burned and used to produce a cheap coffee substitute? So the chiffoniers even collect old crusts, too.'

'Goodness,' Rose said. 'Well, all the more reason to save as much of this baguette as possible.' She took the remaining pieces to add to her parcels of food.

'I must admit that I save whatever I can for them,' Phillip added, smiling. 'It's not much but I like to feel I'm doing something.'

'Ooh, is that dessert?' Lily squealed, as the waiter presented them each with a small dish of crème brulée with a light buttery biscuit on the side.

'So you're not so full after all?' Rose said, raising her eyebrows slightly as Lily picked up the tiny silver spoon to crack the delicious looking layer of burnt sugar on the top.

'I'd always have space for this, Rose,'

Lily replied, grinning. 'It's divine. What were you two talking about anyway and what's a chiffonier? Is it a new style of dress?'

'It really doesn't matter,' Rose said as she cracked the sugar on her own dessert. She exchanged a quiet smile with Phillip, who, for no reason he could pinpoint, other than the early start he'd had that morning, found himself rather weary of the journey so far.

Suddenly he really couldn't wait to arrive at the hotel they'd booked and have a rest.

He took a couple of mouthfuls of his own dessert and creamy and delicious as it was, he realised he'd lost his appetite and his stomach felt bloated and heavy. Subtly he took the biscuit from the plate, and, when no-one was looking, he added it to Rose's little pile of food parcels.

An Old Adversary

Their coach was waiting for them at Calais when the ship docked and Phillip quickly ushered the Banister sisters on board.

'Well, French soil doesn't feel terribly different so far,' Lily remarked, laughing. 'And the weather's just the same!'

She soon quietened down when the coach departed though and even fell asleep.

'Enjoy the peace!' Rose said, though she was smiling fondly at her younger sister and soon closed her eyes, too.

Phillip watched the two sisters rest, their heads so close together again. Lily looked quite angelic with one golden curl brushing her cheek as her head bobbed up and down with the motion of the coach.

At one point he noticed Rose's lips curl into a smile as she slept and he found himself wondering what it was she'd found so amusing. It must have been a very pleasant sort of dream.

It had been a long day of travelling for all concerned and, having dozed on and off himself, Phillip felt relieved when the coachman told them they were finally on the outskirts of Paris.

Darkness had fallen, so the sights would have to wait till the following day.

Phillip was woken by sunbeams streaming through the windows of his elegantly furnished room in Le Grande Hotel, which had been built especially for international guests attending the main exhibition when it opened two years ago in 1867.

He knew he should have pulled the shutters closed the night before but there was something wonderful about letting the early sun shine in. He'd missed the splendour of the Paris mornings.

Phillip had felt a momentary pang for his small but comfortable apartment on the other side of the city, but it would have hardly been appropriate to take the Banister sisters there, and anyway, it only had one bedroom. Plus there was something very luxurious about this upmarket hotel.

Every room had a fireplace in it and the furniture and furnishings were plush and ornate. Everything had been decorated in the fashionable style of Second Empire France.

The sisters seemed rested and ready for the day ahead. Lily was her usual talkative and bright-eyed self over breakfast as she marvelled at the sweetness of the hot chocolate and the deliciousness of the flaky croissants they were served.

She was as stunning as always in her deep emerald morning dress with a ruched bodice which emphasised her tiny frame.

'I don't know how you stay so slim,' Rose commented, mirroring Phillip's own thoughts, as Lily happily accepted a second serving of hot chocolate.

Rose wore a far more modest dress in a delicate white with dusty pink puffed sleeves. She had worn darker colours on every other occasion that they'd met and Phillip thought the lighter shade suited her. She looked younger, somehow, and he could tell she was looking forward to exploring Paris and seeing all the exhibition had to offer.

The sun beat down on the party as they left Le Grande Hotel and stepped out along the Rue Scribe. Both sisters instantly loosened their bonnets and opened their parasols as they began their walk to the Champs de Mar, the large public park, where the exhibition was taking place.

'It'll take around fifty minutes to get there on foot,' Phillip warned the sisters as they set off. 'I can ask the hotel to arrange a coach for us if you would prefer?'

'Nonsense,' Lily replied. 'It's a beautiful day and I want to breathe in as much of Paris as I possibly can.' Rose nodded eagerly in agreement.

Phillip noticed that she was clutching the food parcels from the day before and discreetly nodded to a couple of chiffoniers shifting through items ejected from the well-off households close by, who gratefully accepted the free meal.

He watched as Rose and Lily took in the well-dressed and stylish Parisians as well as the styles of shops and buildings, which, of course, were all new to them.

'French soil definitely feels different now,' Lily announced, laughing. 'I could live here for ever!'

Phillip pointed out notable sights as they walked and explained how the whole of Paris had been redesigned by Emperor Napoleon III, who, whatever your personal opinion of him might be, had undoubtedly changed the land-scape of the capital beyond recognition and had insisted on modernising the city.

New boulevards, markets and the-atres, which had all been built on

101

Napoleon's instructions, were in evidence as they walked the streets in the direction of the Champs de Mars.

'Look, Miss Lily,' Phillip commented as they passed a large and impressive public garden. It was full of deciduous trees thick with new leaves and a carpet of late spring flowers which quivered and danced, as if by magic, in the light spring breeze.

'This is called the Tuileries Garden and has been open to the public ever since the end of the French Revolution.'

'How marvellous,' Lily replied, staring out over the scene. It was full of Parisians taking the early morning air and children rushed about whooping and calling to each other as they played. 'And what's that building over there? Is it a palace?'

'It's the Louvre Art Gallery,' Phillip answered, smiling. 'We shall go another day, if you like.'

'I hope the pictures are bright and fun,' Lily said. 'Not just gloomy old men like you see in most of the fine houses at home.'

'Lily, there are some real masterpieces in there,' Rose cut in. 'It's a great honour to have this opportunity to see them.'

'Look, we're at the river,' Lily squealed, not bothering to reply to her older sister. 'We must be nearly there.'

Phillip felt his own excitement mounting as the three of them crossed the bridge over the River Seine.

A huge rectangular building stood before them in the Champs de Mars. Made of iron and glass and surely a mile in circumference, it could only have been the main exhibition building.

Scores of other smaller buildings were dotted around the rest of the park, which must have covered over 100 acres.

Phillip had seen it all before, of course, but had always been too busy in the embassy to have a look inside on the rare occasions it was open.

He still felt rather bruised and

disappointed to have missed out on seeing the exhibition in 1867, the first time around. A large fountain stood at the front of the main building with several ornate stone angels sitting amidst jets of fast flowing water.

'Oh,' Lily cried, rushing ahead, 'the water looks simply divine. I'm so very warm from all this walking and really must splash my face.'

'Careful,' Phillip heard her sister warn, but there was no stopping Lily as she made her way towards the pool. He, too, felt hot from the exercise and his heart was thumping heavily beneath his waistcoat and shirt.

He could certainly empathise with how Lily was feeling, yet wasn't sure a public fountain was quite the place for freshening up.

Lily was already kneeling by the water when Phillip and Rose caught up with her.

'This is heavenly,' she laughed as she ladled the water in both hands and cascaded it over her face. Soon her eyelashes and bonnet were dripping with tiny droplets of water.

'My, my,' came a rich and well-spoken voice as a striking figure loomed over them. 'What have we here, Monty, a water nymph? Why, you might as well be one of those angels lounging by the pool.'

With a heart stopping thud in his chest, Phillip looked up to see his old enemy and rival, Gordon Pomfret, standing right by the fountain, with a maddening smirk on his chiselled and handsome face.

Change of Mood

Rose looked up to see a young man in fashionable dress and with startling blue eyes standing in front of them. His figure was slight and almost wiry, though he was of a good height. There was something about him which most definitely caught the eye.

His wide and tubular trousers were nicely tailored and his lounging jacket was of a similar quality to Phillip's, though it was deep purple in colour rather than the more conservative grey of their host's.

Like Phillip, this gentleman was clean shaven. He lifted his top hat in a polite greeting to the sisters and in doing so revealed striking blond hair. It reminded Rose of a golden cornfield kissed by a generous late summer sun.

'Allow me to introduce myself to you charming young ladies,' the gentleman said, giving a small bow. 'My name is Gordon Pomfret and I'm delighted to make your acquaintance.'

There was a pause as Rose looked at Lily expecting her to respond for them both. She was, however, frantically and quite self-consciously wiping at her face and bonnet with one of her pocket handkerchiefs. Her cheeks had flushed with those bright spots of pink again.

Phillip had taken a few steps back with a most curious expression on his face, which left Rose feeling utterly bewildered.

'It's a pleasure to meet you, Mr Pomfret,' she said quickly. Clearly she was the only member of their party who was currently capable of speech. 'We are Misses Rose and Lily Banister and I'm presuming you already know our friend, Phillip.'

'Oh, Monty and I are old chums from school,' Mr Pomfret chuckled in reply. He didn't share any of their host's discomfort and was clapping him on the back.

'You're a dark horse, old fellow, turning up here in the company of these two enchanting creatures. Not bad going for a shopkeeper's lad.' He laughed again and poked Phillip good-naturedly in the ribs. He was either impervious or oblivious to the grimace his friend gave in response.

'I had no idea you were back in Paris,' Phillip replied. His voice was as cold as a northern winter and he wouldn't meet Mr Pomfret's eye.

'There's only so much grouse shoot-ing a man can take,' Mr Pomfret said, rolling his eyes languidly. 'And as much as I love the Kentish countryside, it's not often that another chance rolls by to see the great exhibition, though it was exhilarating the first time, I have to say.'

'You went when it opened?' Lily had found her vocal cords now the water from her face had dried off. 'Was it splendid?'

'Exquisite,' Mr Pomfret answered. 'Just wait till you see the Chinese

Pavilion. Isn't it just fabulous, Monty? Oh wait, you didn't get to go, did you? Such a darned shame.'

'Quite,' Phillip replied shortly. 'I suppose some of us had to work.'

'Enough of that,' Mr Pomfret said. He was laughing again but just a little too loudly this time. 'Dear old Monty will pretend to be vexed by me, but really we're the greatest of pals.

'Together at Eton and once again as attachés in the embassy. We're soon to become Second Secretaries once our leave is over. Destiny has bound us together, eh, Monty?'

'Written in the stars,' Phillip replied, his voice heavy with sarcasm. 'Oxford was the only time I had a break,' he went on.

'Well, one can't make perfect choices all the time, Monty,' Mr Pomfret said. All four of them were now making their way over to the exhibition building. 'I went to Cambridge, of course, the best university on the planet.'

'I'm not getting into that debate

again,' Phillip said. 'We'll be arguing for the rest of our lives.'

'Just because we beat you at the boat race,' Mr Pomfret answered with glee. 'I was the cox, of course, a great role for a whippet like me!'

'I seem to recall that it was Oxford who won the latest boat race,' Phillip replied quickly, though Rose could tell that he didn't wish to be drawn any further into the conversation. Still, Mr Pomfret also seemed to have lost interest in the discussion.

Lily, as usual, had rushed ahead and their new companion was staring after her, as if momentarily spellbound. Lily's magic had clearly struck again.

The party of four approached the lengthy queue that had already formed at the entrance.

'Goodness, this will take hours,' Lily cried, deflating a little and looking around for a seat.

'Be patient,' Rose replied. 'It'll be worth it.'

Mr Pomfret, however, had momentarily disappeared but was back in sight within seconds and was beckoning the party to come with him.

'My father knows the chairman of the exhibition committee,' he explained as Lily whooped in surprise and delight at their escape from the boredom of the queue.

'Let's go into the park first,' Mr Pomfret said, picking up his pace to keep up with Lily who was as energetic as always. 'It really is a sight to behold.'

The two of them walked several paces ahead of Rose and Phillip.

'This is most exciting for us,' she remarked as they walked.

'And me,' he responded as he turned to smile at her. Rose couldn't help but notice, however, that ever since Mr Pomfret had joined their party, their host hadn't been himself.

The effervescent confidence with which he'd educated the sisters on Second Empire Paris and the fizz of his enthusiasm for the outing had all but evaporated and his entire demeanour had very visibly drooped.

His smile certainly didn't extend to his eyes, which now looked hooded and grim. Phillip's shoulders were rather hunched, too. They had never looked that way before.

Rose wasn't sure what to say. The whole affair had turned quite uncomfortable. Personally she couldn't see what was quite so objectionable about the newcomer. He was charismatic, that was for sure, and had already presented himself as a knowledgeable and helpful guide.

Rose wouldn't have minded queuing with everyone else but had to admit that Mr Pomfret's intervention was very welcome. The man was something of a show-off, that was clear, and there was obviously some rivalry between the two of them, but that didn't seem enough of a reason for Phillip to be so visibly disturbed by the appearance of his colleague.

In fact, Mr Pomfret had been warm

and gracious in his approach to Phillip and Rose couldn't quite believe that their host had been so cool in response.

She didn't want her opinion of Phillip to change so quickly and kept an open mind, but still, the matter was somewhat awkward and she hoped his melancholy mood would make a swift recovery.

Inside the Exhibition

On arrival into the park, however, all such thoughts went on hold. Rose felt her soul leap in wonder and all five of her senses tingle with anticipation as she took in the scene.

A multi-coloured fairground of pleasure and luxury lay before them as mouth-watering smells of spices, sweetmeats and sugar filled the pleasant spring air.

The park looked even bigger than it had done from the outside and the attractions spread as far as the eye could see.

Vendors were selling their wares at stalls all over the grounds. Elegant-looking folk in the finest clothes swanned around as conjurers, clowns, acrobats and jugglers bounced about entertaining the visitors.

Somewhere an orchestra must have

been playing as lilting notes floated around the grounds, though Rose couldn't see the musicians anywhere.

Then there were the exhibits themselves. Rose spied sculptures, artwork, extravagant water features and intriguing looking inventions comprising of intricate metalwork, carved wood and ceramics.

She saw what must be the Chinese Pavilion which Mr Pomfret had referred to earlier. It was an ornate structure painted in the palest blue, with bright pillars and a golden roof. There was even a full-size Gothic cathedral in the park plus a tall and thin wooden structure resembling a lighthouse.

'Rose, wake up!' It would seem that Lily had been trying to get Rose's attention for some time. She had been too awestruck to notice. 'We're going to look round,' Lily informed her, taking her none too gently by the arm.

In a heartbeat, Rose found herself swept along in Lily's storm of elation and joy. She, too, was overwhelmed by the brilliance of it all, though couldn't help but wish she could have taken as long as she needed to absorb every wonder-filled tiny detail.

'The exhibition is designed to celebrate nature's bounty and transform it into universal harmony for the human race,' Mr Pomfret explained as they paused by wicker hampers packed full of fresh alpine produce. There were packs of golden butter, creamy cheese and crusty farmhouse bread as well as glass bottles of elderflower juice, which looked very similar to lemonade.

'You know everything,' Lily gasped, staring at their new companion. She made no attempt whatsoever to mask her admiration and awe.

'It's written in the exhibition programme,' Phillip replied from slightly behind the other three. Rose noticed that his syllables were shorter and more clipped sounding than before and when she turned to look at him, she saw that his eyes were narrowed and glinting, she supposed, with suppressed rage.

Mr Pomfret made no further comment, and continued to lead the way round the various exhibits.

They went inside several of the smaller buildings where they admired more artwork, artefacts and newly designed furniture.

Mr Pomfret generally had a gem of wisdom or interesting thought about each one, but as interesting as it was, Rose felt herself becoming increasingly ill at ease.

Phillip made no further comment, but she could almost feel the heat of his anguish radiating from him and his ears were as red as a mini furnace. Like a dormant volcano, he was dangerously quiet and Rose felt very unnerved by it all.

She had to admit that Mr Pomfret had rather taken over proceedings and was acting as though she and Lily had been his guests all along. Plus, she couldn't help but note that Lily had barely taken her eyes off their new companion ever since he had arrived on the scene.

She had to consider that their host might be concerned that Mr Pomfret was something of a rival for Lily's affections. Perhaps this would explain his unfamiliar behaviour and the barely disguised hostility in his manner.

Still, surely he knew Lily well enough by now to understand that she was a wild and impulsive young lady who was easily distracted by a little attention and a well-placed compliment here and there, especially from a handsome gentleman of high social standing.

If Phillip represented a higher station to them, then Mr Pomfret belonged in a different stratosphere altogether.

Rose had already heard him telling Lily of his family's country residence in Kent and their London town-house in Mayfair. She had a feeling he was landed gentry.

Next, the party headed for the main exhibition hall, to marvel at yet more exhibits which ranged from the industrious, the absurd and the downright beautiful.

They passed china dolls in immaculate silken clothing with rosy laughing faces and opulent doll's-houses full of finely crafted furniture and fittings, so perfect in their construction and attention to detail and style that they looked fit for miniature royalty.

They saw richly patterned Persian carpets and India rubber baths. It was as if every nation in the world had collected the best they had to offer to display at this proud and expansive celebration of worldwide progress and achievement.

'Goodness, I'm quite exhausted and just gasping for some refreshment,' Lily announced, collapsing on a nearby armchair.

'Good gracious, Lily,' Rose cried, her insides churning with panic. 'That's not a seat for visitors, it's an exhibit!' Lily leaped up like a firecracker.

The two gentleman looked almost as

shocked as Rose, though Mr Pomfret quickly recovered and steered them away from the chair and the accusing eye of an exhibition official nearby.

Rose took a quick look back as they hastily left the scene of the crime. The chair, which was expertly carved and polished in a deep and rich gloss, looked mercifully unharmed as did the golden plush cushion on the seat.

'I never even supposed it was part of the show,' she could hear Lily saying to the gentlemen. She seemed to have calmed down, but Rose could tell by the jittery way she was giggling, that Lily was still quite embarrassed by her faux pas.

'Well, we can take a hint,' Mr Pomfret replied. 'I recall that there was a rather special Parisian café some-where around here during the last exhibition. Let's try to find it.'

The party of four followed the purple of Mr Pomfret's lounging jacket as they weaved through the crowds of fairgoers.

Sure enough, tucked away in one of

the furthest corners of the exhibition hall was a delightful looking café called Maison de Delicieux.

It had a beautifully high ceiling, long mirrors with gold plated frames and fashionable paintings on the walls.

It looked fresh from the boulevards of Paris and Rose couldn't help but stare as she took everything in.

Mr Pomfret conducted a hurried exchange in French with the waitress. Rose struggled to catch all of it but it would seem they were expecting some important visitors soon and had to keep most of the tables free.

Mr Pomfret was as charming as ever but also fairly insistent — Rose was sure she heard him mention his father and their connections to the exhibition — and eventually two smaller tables several feet apart were produced.

Rose hesitated when she saw Lily and Mr Pomfret select their table and sit down. Surely the two ladies should sit together. Wasn't this frightfully improper? Still, Lily was hardly on the other side of Paris. Rose could even hear her ordering some hot chocolate despite Mr Pomfret's encouraging her to try the coffee.

Adjusting her seat slightly so Lily would never be out of her sight, Rose smiled at Phillip who had sat down at her table, too. She tried to relax and continue to enjoy the day out, which already felt worlds away from their mostly quiet life in Upper Wimpole Street.

Phillip exhaled deeply and they both ordered coffee. He took several quick sips of his once it arrived and looked visibly refreshed by the drink, which, Rose would have to agree, as she took a sip of her own, was remarkably good.

She watched as Phillip's shoulders began to relax and could almost see the tension disappearing from them. Some time away from Mr Pomfret, albeit fleeting, was working wonders.

'I remember when I called at your house that first time, that you spoke of your liking of Poe,' he started. 'Which of his is your favourite work?'

Before long Rose was talking animatedly about her enjoyment of the eerily supernatural poem, 'The Raven' and his haunting short story, 'The Fall Of The House Of Usher'. They discussed Dickens, too, and before long had entered into a lively debate about which book better represented London life today, 'Little Dorrit' or 'Great Expectations'.

They were so busy talking that Rose didn't notice Mr Pomfret rise to greet these 'important visitors' the waitress had referred to and it was only the squeal of delight from Lily that finally prompted her to look over.

Mr Pomfret and Lily were in conversation with an intense looking gentleman in fine dress. Rose could only hope and pray that Lily was conducting herself in an appropriate manner and that Mr Pomfret had the good sense to censor any silly remarks as he translated for her.

'You'll simply never guess who I just

met, Rose,' Lily cried as the party left the café and went back out to the exhibition. 'Only Monsieur Edouard Manet! The great artist.'

'Gracious,' Rose was impressed. She didn't ask if Lily had heard of him before this encounter. She rather suspected she hadn't but to ask the question now would have been unnecessarily unkind.

'He wants to paint me!' Lily giggled, jumping up and down. 'Oh, the excitement, Rose. I'm to be a model.'

Rose laughed and exclaimed with her sister though couldn't help but hope the artist was just being polite. She wasn't sure she could cope with Lily becoming an artist's muse.

Moreover, they were due to travel to the French Rivera in a couple of days, so surely there wouldn't be time.

They spent the rest of the day looking round some more of the exhibition and ate a late luncheon at another of the cafés in the main exhibition hall. Clearly they would need to return for at least another full day as it was simply impossible to take everything in during a single visit.

The coffee interlude had vastly improved Phillip's spirits and he was almost his old self again by the end of the day, much to Rose's relief.

*   *   *

The sun was low in the sky when they finally emerged from the exhibition. Once again, Lily declared herself 'exhausted' and Mr Pomfret promptly waved over a coach which turned out to belong to him.

It had comfortable velvet seating which the sisters happily sank into and if there hadn't been so many interesting sights to see from the window, Rose was pretty sure she would have fallen asleep.

Mr Pomfret's coach dropped them off at Le Grande Hotel and he insisted on escorting them right into the building.

Phillip was once again looking tense

and annoyed, especially when Mr Pomfret invited them all to take dinner with him than evening.

'Why don't you two go upstairs?' Phillip suggested, without accepting or declining Mr Pomfret's offer. Lily was visibly drooping with tiredness but had perked up by the idea of dinner.

'Thank you both so much for such a splendid day,' she said before taking her leave. Her gratitude was clearly aimed at both gentlemen, but she still couldn't take her eyes off their new friend.

It wasn't until they were inside their hotel room that Lily announced she'd left her parasol in the lobby.

'I'll go and get it,' Rose said, somewhat unnecessarily as Lily had already curled up on her bed.

'Oh, you are a dear,' Lily replied sleepily, wrapping herself in one of the warm soft blankets. 'I'll just catch forty winks before we dress for dinner.'

Rose made her way back down to the lobby, pausing to admire the Impressionist artwork on the walls and enjoying the view from the large windows as she passed by.

She still couldn't quite get over the sumptuous style of the hotel or believe that she and Lily were guests there. It all felt like a fanciful dream.

When she reached the lobby, however, she stopped short. Their two gentleman companions were still standing there and though she was out of earshot, Rose could tell by their expressions and gestures that their conversation was far from friendly.

Quickly, she sidled up to the chaise longue nearby, where she could see Lily's parasol propped up against the side. Thankfully she was out of the direct vision of the two men but she was near enough to overhear.

'Stay away, Pomfret,' Phillip hissed. 'No good will come of this, I'm telling you. Just stay well away.'

Rose was too worried about being seen to wait around to hear Mr Pomfret's reply, but, once again, her heart was full of unease as she made her way back to the hotel room and Lily.

Not the Time or Place

'Confounded man! What rotten luck!' Phillip said aloud.

He still couldn't believe that the blasted Pomfret had turned up at the exhibition of all places and right at the beginning of their trip.

His head was in turmoil as he trod heavily up the stairs and back to his hotel room. He had managed to keep the brute at bay for tonight at least, but he knew that it was only a matter of time before he would return. His words carried little weight when it came to the strength of Pomfret and his will.

Not only that, Phillip was uncomfortably aware of the influence he carried at the embassy and what the impact might be of any disagreement with him.

Officially, he and Pomfret were on the same level, but everyone knew that it only took a click of Pomfret's father's fingers to change everything. Family ties still carried far more power than merit in the diplomatic service.

It didn't matter how much money Montgomery's store brought in, Phillip would always be the 'shopkeeper's lad' in the eyes of those in charge. Pomfret knew it, too. He wasn't a man to cross, however much one might dislike him.

★   ★   ★

Dinner that evening was a quiet affair. Lily couldn't hide her disappointment when Phillip informed them that Mr Pomfret wouldn't be joining them after all and even the four-course meal Phillip had arranged for them at a fine restaurant near the Arc de Triomphe failed to lift her spirits.

He had never seen her eat so little and as soon as they had finished, Lily announced that she and Rose would be retiring back to the hotel and bed. Rose, too, seemed subdued, and he was rather glad that the whole day was over.

130

'You're overreacting, old chap,' Pomfret had replied when Phillip tried to warn him off in the lobby.

'Am I?' Phillip retorted. 'You seemed intent on taking over everything today! Can I remind you that my travel companions are not mere playthings to toy with, but my friends? I would ask you to respect that.'

'My dear Monty, I have nothing but the deepest regard for those delightful young ladies and sought nothing but the pleasure of their company.'

'Hmm.' Phillip remained unconvinced. Pomfret's record was far from flawless when it came to the treatment of ladies and Phillip didn't trust him a jot.

'Don't look so doubtful, my friend,' Pomfret continued. 'I just thought I might be able to offer them a few perks as a result of my contacts. I certainly didn't mean to steal the show. Look, I'll duck out tonight to show you that I'm sorry. How's that?'

Phillip had had no choice but to

shake his old rival's hand and take his leave, but he didn't feel reassured at all.

★ ★ ★

Sure enough, Mr Pomfret was waiting for the party in the hotel lobby as soon as they had finished their breakfast the following morning.

'I thought you might like a lift back to Le Champs de Mars.' He grinned, with a gesture to his fancy coach waiting outside.

Phillip wanted to decline but on hearing Lily's burst of delight, he felt the words stick in his throat and before long the four of them were being ushered into Mr Pomfret's coach and transported back to the splendour of the Paris Exhibition.

The view of the park was just as bewitching as the previous day and, for a moment, Phillip let himself be transported back to that fairy-tale wonderland created by this startling and magnificent world fair.

132

There were the same culinary smells, cheers from the crowd, melodic music from an unseen orchestra and bright bursts of colour from exhibits and entertainers alike. It was all so enchanting that Phillip felt his worries float off into the warm and fragrant air, until he heard Rose speak up next to him.

'Mr Montgomery? Shouldn't we follow Lily? She and Mr Pomfret are heading off.'

Darn it, of course they were! There was never a moment's peace with that wilful young brute!

'Why yes, grand idea,' Phillip heard himself say in reply, despite his inner thoughts.

He could see the sunshine yellow of Lily's bonnet in the crowds ahead of them. It was like a bright little beacon lighting the way. Thankfully, the pair had come to a standstill by a popular stall exhibiting fine clothes.

Phillip could see Lily bobbing around in excitement and trying to get a closer look. No doubt Pomfret would find some way of whisking her to the front any second.

Phillip and Rose slowed their pace and he wondered if she shared his lack of enthusiasm for staring at the latest fashions. She was always nicely dressed but didn't quite seem to share her younger sister's frantic fascination with clothes.

Today she wore a light green day dress which was dotted with tiny white flowers. Her shining hair, once again, was spilling from her bonnet and framed her face in pretty curls.

'Well, at least we can see them from here,' she commented as they came to a stop.

An entertainer on sky-high stilts strolled past them. Her face was plastered in white paint and a black pencil had been used to extenuate her eyes. Both Phillip and Rose stopped to gaze up at her as she waved to the visitors and blew air kisses from pursed ruby lips.

'Mr Montgomery,' Rose started after

134

the entertainer had moved on. A frown had appeared on her brow and she looked rather uncomfortable.

'Yes?' Phillip felt worried. He hoped he hadn't done anything wrong.

'I couldn't help but notice that you seemed a little anxious and preoccupied yesterday and,' she paused, colouring slightly as she spoke, 'I think it may have something to do with Mr Pomfret. Tell me, is everything quite all right?'

Phillip opened his mouth to speak. To share his feelings about Pomfret would be such an incredible relief and he was tempted to do so there and then. He had been wanting to vent about that ratbag ever since his Eton years and although his parents had listened sympathetically enough, there was a limit to how much he could say.

He was acutely aware, however, that Rose was his guest and his role was to act as a guide and to make sure she was having a pleasant and engaging time.

It would be most improper to tell her the truth about Pomfret and Phillip's personal feelings towards him. It would worry her, for a start, which would be most unfair. He couldn't bear to spoil this trip for her when she'd clearly enjoyed it so far.

In any case, they would be off to the French Riviera the day after tomorrow. If he could keep the lout at bay till then, then this most unpleasant interlude would be in the past, exactly where it belonged.

He was in the middle of reassuring Rose when they both started at a squeal of joy which was so unmistakably Lily, they would have recognised it from the bottom of the sea.

They looked over to see that she had spied a man selling ladies' gloves in all those snazzy colours she talked of so passionately and was now rushing over to him with delight.

Rose rolled her eyes but turned to give Phillip a gentle smile as they went over to the vendor, too. Her mind seemed at rest for now.

True Colours

Lily and Pomfret stayed close by for the rest of the morning and they all took luncheon together in a different restaurant in the main exhibition hall.

As usual, Pomfret dominated the conversation at the table with his talk of the splendid balls his family would host back home and although Phillip nodded along politely, inside, he was using this unexpected stretch of time to collect his thoughts.

He couldn't allow Rose to worry any more or for Lily to be led even further down this disastrous road to defeat. It was time for him to stand up to Pomfret as best as he could in the circumstances and take back control as the host of this holiday.

'So the exhibition has been truly splendid, but I propose a change tomorrow. It's our last day in Paris, after all, and I would like to show you some more of the city,' he announced once dessert was over and coffee was being served.

He spoke politely but firmly and didn't stop to let any counter and most likely more attractive alternatives get a chance to get brought to the table.

Everyone looked slightly surprised that he'd spoken up after being so quiet for the majority of the meal.

'I think we should take a look round the Louvre in the morning and then make our way to Montmartre in the afternoon. I don't know if you ladies recall me speaking of it when I first called on you in London but I'd love for you both to see the views from up there. It is quite my favourite spot in the whole of Paris.'

'Yes, I remember,' Rose said, nodding, whilst Lily shrugged in happy indifference.

'Sounds marvellous,' she concurred. Phillip couldn't miss her turning her head just slightly to smile at Pomfret who was sitting next to her, clearly assuming that he would be joining them, too.

'It does indeed sound most enjoyable,' Pomfret said. 'I'm afraid I won't be joining you, though.'

Phillip suppressed a cry of joy. The relief he felt on hearing this news was immense and he felt lighter and happier almost instantly.

'I have a long-standing engagement with another embassy chum tomorrow morning,' Pomfret continued, 'and an afternoon of croquet planned with him, his wife and a few others in the afternoon.

'I had meant to mention it earlier, actually, but as usual, the glory of the exhibits alongside the exquisite charm of the company, quite swept me away.'

Phillip resisted the urge to roll his eyes. He could hear the insincerity dripping off Pomfret's words, but Lily was utterly oblivious.

'Ooh, how fabulous! I've never played croquet before,' Lily said brightly, turning to flash Mr Pomfret a dazzling smile.

There was an expectant pause. Pomfret shuffled slightly in his seat and, for the first time in all the years that Phillip had known him, looked slightly ill at ease.

'And one day you'll learn, Miss Lily,' he said eventually, returning her smile, which most definitely didn't reach his eyes. 'I'd wager you'd be rather good at it, too.'

Lily still didn't seem to have fully realised that no invitation was forthcoming and began asking Pomfret how the rules of croquet worked. It was only when they settled the bill and rose for one last look round the exhibition that the disappointment really set in.

In her yellow and apricot gown and bonnet, she looked like a wilted hothouse flower that had been plucked from the tropics and dropped on a dim winter lawn.

She trailed behind them and despite

Mr Pomfret's attempts to steer the conversation back to pleasant ground, she remained sullen and visibly disgruntled.

Phillip felt for Lily. He had been on the receiving end of Pomfret on numerous occasions himself and offered his full empathy to anyone else who was unfortunate enough to be hurt by him, too.

He knew exactly who Pomfret was referring to when he spoke of his 'other embassy chum' with whom he had this long-standing engagement.

It was Robert Chadwick, a high-flying diplomat and close friend of Pomfret's father. He had been personally acquainted with Viscount Palmerston who was Prime Minister when they had started at the embassy.

In fact, Phillip felt sure that it was Pomfret's father with his aristocratic connections that gave his son safe passage into the diplomatic service whilst the likes of Phillip had to work for every penny they made.

Phillip would never be invited to such an exclusive affair. It was clearly some kind of inner-circle soirée requiring a direct invitation from the host.

Phillip was so accustomed to being pushed out of such gatherings that it ceased to worry him any more and he knew he wouldn't enjoy it anyway, but to view Lily's reaction to the sting made old wounds smart all over again and indignation on her behalf surged through him.

After all, Pomfret who felt at liberty to turn up uninvited on all their planned activities had simply dropped his new friends like hot coals at the first sniff of a better offer.

Still, Phillip pondered, as they began to make preparations to return to the hotel, perhaps it was better for Lily to experience the true nature of Pomfret so early in their acquaintance.

Far better for her to learn of his character now, than to be burned later on and suffer goodness knows how much damage to her reputation.

Men like Pomfret with their charming exteriors, titled connections and aristocratic roots saw ladies like Lily as easy prey; mere toys to pick up and put down at their choosing. Phillip didn't want this for Lily. Her soul was too pure for such carelessness.

He wished with all his heart that he could simply ban Pomfret from any further dealings with the party without any further ado. After all, if he told the Banister sisters all that he knew about Pomfret, neither of them would ever want anything to do with him again.

Although, of course, to anger or to slight that beast of a man, would most likely mean a pistol shot through his career, as if Phillip were nothing but an ill-fated pheasant desperately swooping for cover on the Pomfret family's land.

He would risk everything he had worked for to save Lily's honour, but it was somewhat comforting to know that she'd come to that conclusion herself, without costing Phillip his job.

Lily was still looking crestfallen when Pomfret's coach dropped them back at the hotel. Clearly all efforts to cheer her up had continued to fall flat.

'Miss Lily . . . ' Pomfret called when she turned to walk through the large glass doors at the entrance of the hotel with Rose.

Lily turned and raised her chin slightly. Her eyes were glassy and her face solemn. Pomfret beckoned her back to him, and though she hesitated for a moment, Phillip was disappointed to see that it didn't take long for her to walk over. He had hoped the rejection would be enough to alienate Lily entirely.

'Yes?' she asked coldly once she reached him.

Phillip watched as Pomfret leaned down to whisper something in her ear. His heart sank even further as the ghost of a smile returned to Lily's lips as she nodded and shyly pushed a wisp of hair from her eyes. Perhaps they weren't quite finished with Gordon Pomfret just yet.

Exploring Paris

Phillip tried to push all thoughts of the whisper from his mind the following day.

The relief of a prolonged stretch of time without Pomfret was like a long hot bath at the end of a bitterly cold walk on a rugged mountainside. It was almost as if he could breathe properly again.

As planned, they spent an enjoyable morning at the Louvre. He showed the sisters notable works such as the Mona Lisa and St John the Baptist, explaining some of the history behind each painting, too.

He got the impression that Rose would have lingered for longer at each painting given the opportunity, but she was moved along at a rapid pace by Lily, who had regained her usual energy and appeared refreshed by a night's rest.

'It's such a shame to be indoors when it's another glorious day,' she commented at luncheon, which they'd taken in a pleasant restaurant within the grand Louvre building.

'We've seen such masterpieces though, Lily,' Rose replied, taking a sip of water. The waiter had served thinly cut roast beef in a sauce that was bursting with flavour.

The absence of Pomfret from the table made every mouthful all the more delicious and Phillip savoured every bite.

'It's a once-in-a-lifetime experience, I know,' Lily said, mimicking the sincerity of Rose's voice slightly, but winking at her sister at the same time.

'Well, let's go up to Montmartre after our meal, as I suggested yesterday, and make the most of our last day in Paris,' Phillip said. He was sure the sun would shine just a little brighter now that Pomfret had left their party — for good, with a bit of luck.

★ ★ ★

The sun beat down on Phillip and the sisters as they made their way to Montmartre on foot.

The ladies seemed glad of their parasols and the slight breeze gave them all some relief. The walk was pleasant though and Phillip stopped to point out landmarks of interest and, once again, did his best in his efforts as a guide.

The climb up the hill, however, proved tiring for everybody and Lily insisted on collapsing rather dramatically on a bench halfway to the top.

'It's not a hill, it's a mountain,' she moaned as Rose tried to coax her back up and Phillip called by a house to ask for a cup of cold water to hydrate her.

It was only his promise of a delightful little patisserie at the top that persuaded her to carry on. Phillip felt his own heart quicken as they climbed the steep incline. It was a walk he knew well but he could feel the lack of practice as his breathing became more laboured and his legs began to tire. Rose had some colour to her cheeks but appeared cheerful enough whilst Lily continued to protest.

'Was it worth it, ladies?' Phillip asked, when they finally reached the top and looked out at the vast and sprawling capital beneath them. The houses looked like a toy town and the people, tiny dolls. For once Lily was quite speechless.

'How beautiful,' Rose murmured as she turned to take everything in. They gazed at the pretty windmills, stark against the royal blue sky and marvelled at the quaint winding roads and tiny terraces.

'It's like a country village within a huge city,' Rose said, clearly as charmed by the place as Phillip had been when he visited for the first time.

'And everyone looks so artistic,' Lily added, as she peered at a refined-looking lady sketching at a window inside one of the houses.

Phillip kept his promise and they

spent an enjoyable half hour or so in the patisserie eating dainty puff pastry tarts topped with fresh strawberries and cream, all washed down with sumptuous hot chocolate.

'I'll have to roll back down the hill,' Lily giggled.

The walk back was much easier and they all felt revived by the refreshments. Phillip wasn't sure if it was the sugar from the cakes, the bright sun overhead or the heady scent of the cherry blossoms they passed as they walked by, but his head was spinning in a delightful mixture of relaxation and anticipation.

Finally he'd had the chance to impress the sisters without being bettered by Pomfret every time he'd opened his mouth. He wasn't sure he would ever forget Rose's face as she gazed down on Paris from the top of the hill. Her wonder mirrored his own.

★　★　★

'Home, sweet home,' Lily sang, once they reached the hotel. There was time for a quick rest before dressing for dinner.

'Now don't you all look jolly,' came a voice from one of the easy chairs in the lobby. 'You ladies can certainly keep a man waiting.'

Lily gave out a peal of delighted laughter whilst Phillip felt the magic of the day float off in the early evening breeze. He might have known this would happen. Pomfret rose looking remarkably pleased with himself, in a lazy sort of a way.

He was wearing an expensive-looking mauve waistcoat over a crisp white shirt and pinstripe trousers. His top hat sat at a rather jaunty angle and he took it off to address them.

'I thought you were busy all day,' Phillip remarked. He could feel the chill in his voice.

'I was, but I rather missed our new friends,' Pomfret answered languidly. 'And anyway, I have a little announcement to make.'

Phillip took a sideways glance at Lily. She was beaming from ear to ear. He had a feeling she knew what was coming as his mind took him back to that whisper at the end of the previous day.

'I fancy a little trip to the Riviera myself,' Pomfret went on as all Phillip's worst fears bubbled up in his face.

'My father knows some thoroughly splendid people in Nice, who would be delighted to entertain us. There will be seaside picnics, cricket, croquet and dancing, not to mention the stunning views around the bay.'

Lily was visibly fizzing with excitement and Rose was smiling too. Phillip wasn't sure there was any colour left in his face as he heard the animated voices of the others as they made plans for the rest of the holiday.

It wasn't until after Rose gently steered Lily to their room to dress for dinner that he finally found his voice.

'You promised me, Pomfret!' he

hissed. 'You said you would leave Miss Lily alone.'

'What can I say, Monty? I'm utterly captivated by her.' Pomfret had the grace to look slightly embarrassed. 'I say, old chap, I think we've got ourselves into a bit of a muddle here. Do you mean to say you're courting Miss Lily?'

'Well, yes, but that's not . . . ' Phillip heard the hesitation in his voice and evidently Pomfret did, too.

'Gracious, Monty,' Pomfret replied, raising an eyebrow as he spoke. 'I'm terribly sorry and all that, but you know, from where I'm standing, I'd wager you were slightly keener on Rose.'

A Long Journey Begins

A letter was waiting for the Banisters when Rose and Lily rose on the following day and went downstairs for their last breakfast at Le Grande Hotel. There were two folded sheets inside the envelope.

Thankfully, Lily was so caught up in her mission to enjoy every mouthful of her final croissants and hot chocolate, despite Rose telling her several times that there'd be such things in Nice, too, that she didn't chatter too much and Rose had a welcome opportunity to enjoy the letter in peace. Phillip had yet to surface from his room, which was out of character for him.

Saturday 2nd May 1869
40 Upper Wimpole Street, London.
My dear daughters,
    I trust you are both well and the

154

journey to France went smoothly.
Lily, I hope you are conducting yourself in an appropriate manner and
managing not to show us Banisters
up in the presence of such genteel
company.

I pray that you are finding enough
palatable food to eat and that it is not
unsettling your stomachs. I hear the
French use enormous amounts of
garlic and cream in their cookery and
one feels quite debilitated at the very
idea.

I shall ask Nell to prepare a boiled
joint for when you return with some
plain potatoes. You will both be glad
of something familiar, I am sure. I
must say the house is rather quiet
without you both, especially you,
Lily. Rose, I am enclosing a letter
which recently arrived from Julia.

Stay well. Your papa sends his
best.

Your loving Mama.

Rose smiled quietly to herself and felt

an unexpected burst of love for her mother. She then picked up the second sheet.

Monday 26th April 1869
High Tides, Brighton.
My dear Rose,

I do hope this letter finds you well. Mama tells me you and Lily are off to France with a dashing diplomat. How wonderfully exciting, Rose! Of course, Barty and I holidayed all over Europe during our honeymoon. I do wish you had told me of your trip, beforehand, as I could have given you all manner of handy hints and travel tips but I gather from Mama that the whole thing happened rather quickly. Something to do with Lily's young man's mother taking ill all of a sudden, so you were required to take her place as chaperone. Well, it is a wonderful opportunity for you to see some of the world, Rose. How jolly for you!

I am feeling quite enormous. There is still two months to go until our third child arrives and it feels like an eternity, especially as the heat of the summer will soon be upon us.

It is no fun being heavy with child in a maternity corset at any time of year. In the meantime Ernest and Blanche continue to test us with their incessant questions and their constant shouting and running around. I fear they drive their nurse, Martha, quite round the twist.

Ernest is nearing five years old and will soon require a governess to add a formal structure of education to his care and prepare him for Eton, where his father is determined he will go to school, when the time comes.

Dear Martha is a kind soul but I fear she lacks the qualifications for promotion to this role. I am quite at a loss for what to do. I am loath to offer employment to a stranger.

The trust one places in the nur-
turing of one's children is beyond
compare, plus I have other concerns
on my mind.

Dear Rose, I know I can speak
frankly to you, as my oldest friend.
One does hear stories of illicit liai-
sons between the governess and the
master of the house.

Barty would not betray me, I am
sure, but still, it is not a risk I am
minded to take. To be honest, Rose,
I would prefer the governess to
have, shall we say, a plainer face
than most, though I hardly suppose
I can specify this on an advertise-
ment. The pressures of family life
are quite ghastly, Rose. You have no
idea!

Do write back and tell me of your
travels. How I envy your carefree
life!

Send my love to Lily.
Your friend, Julia.

Carefree life? Rose couldn't help but

feel a slight sense of frustration by Julia's assumption that everything was easy for her. At present nothing felt straightforward at all.

★   ★   ★

They had now departed and waved a fond farewell to Le Grande Hotel and Paris. It was the first dull day of the holiday and imposing clouds hung over the city. They all felt somewhat glad that the less pleasant weather had come whilst they were travelling.

Mr Pomfret had, once again, offered his own coach for the journey and Phillip, when he finally appeared at breakfast had accepted it, though he didn't look happy at all.

The plush seats in Mr Pomfret's coach were remarkably comfortable, but nothing could stop the jolts from the potholes in the ground or ease the tension in the atmosphere, which was as sharp as a bed of needles.

Lily, of course, was chattering nineteen to the dozen but the input from the other three was sparse. Mr Pomfret, who was sitting opposite her, nodded and smiled in the right places whilst Phillip next to him stared out of the window in silence.

Rose was now fairly sure that the reason their host was upset was because Mr Pomfret had taken his place in Lily's affections.

She had tried to feel reassured after their conversation at the exhibition but was once again feeling concerned. The last thing anyone wanted was the two so-called friends coming to blows over Lily.

If Mr Pomfret had truly usurped him in her sister's heart, then surely Phillip should bow out gracefully and accept the situation, as unfortunate as it might be. All the characteristics Phillip had displayed so far were indicative of the perfect gentleman who would accept such defeat with a rueful smile, with the exception of this attitude towards his supposed friend.

Rose found herself hoping they got through the remainder of the holiday without the tension coming to a head. She wasn't keen on confrontation.

Her thoughts turned to Julia's letter. If ever there was a time to present herself as the perfect solution to the problem of securing a suitable governess, it was now.

She even wondered if Julia was hinting in her letter that Rose would be the perfect choice, though of course it was hard to tell.

Yes, she would write to Julia as soon as this trip was nearing its close. As much as this plan made perfect sense, Rose felt her mood sink a little further at the thought of the years ahead, and, as if reading her mind, a few spots of rain began to splash against the coach windows.

The dark clouds had followed them from Paris. It looked set to be a miserable day all over France. Rose couldn't quite work out why she felt this way, as she stared out of the window and watched as the damp countryside rolled by.

She was fairly sure that Julia's children were generally very well behaved and that their mother's complaints were mostly habitual rather than founded on any real truth. She knew she would enjoy the teaching, too. So why did the very idea of a new life in Brighton make her feel so melancholy?

Thoughts of the last few days in Paris whirled round in her head. She had never had so many opportunities before — the travelling and new experiences were extremely enjoyable but her mind kept taking her back, most specifically to the chiffoniers, rooting through rubbish, in search of cast out treasures.

Rose turned from the window. Lily was continuing to chat to Mr Pomfret and Phillip appeared to be having a nap. His face still looked strained and there were grey circles around his eyes. Rose found herself studying him. She

162

had a feeling he hadn't slept well last night.

Just then and without any warning at all, Phillip suddenly sat up and opened his eyes very wide and for a moment Rose was locked in his gaze. His expression was impossible to read, but Rose sensed he wanted to tell her something.

Feeling self-conscious, she let her eyes drop and as she turned to look back out of the window, a train of thoughts whizzed through her head, which made her feel quite dizzy with confusion.

Eventually she closed her eyes too and tried to unwind from all that was puzzling her.

A Breath of Fresh Air

The party broke the journey at Auxerre, where they stayed for a night in a hotel booked by Phillip before they set off. They would need to stop three times on their way down to Nice, such was the length of the journey.

The travelling was tiring and they had a quiet supper before retiring to bed fairly early. Even Lily had quietened down and seemed in need of a rest. They had planned on rising at dawn in order to make good progress the following day.

* * *

'Oh this journey is tiresome,' Lily announced soon after they'd set off the next morning. The sun beat down and yesterday's rain was forgotten already. It was somewhat galling to be cooped up all day in a coach, when the weather was so beautiful outdoors.

'Why couldn't we have travelled by train?' she asked. 'It would have been faster, surely.'

'Not in France, I'm afraid,' Mr Pomfret replied. 'Their railroads aren't nearly as advanced as ours. I don't even know if the line stretches as far as Nice and if it does, it's most likely goods trains only.'

'Oh, I had no idea,' Rose said.

'Well, they were grappling with the Napoleonic Wars whilst we were busy building our network,' Mr Pomfret said with a shrug. 'They may be ahead of us with their cuisine but we're winning on railways.'

'Well, it's taking ever such a long time,' Lily said with a sigh. 'Do say we can have a nice walk tomorrow morning before we get started, especially if the weather stays like this. Where is it we're staying tonight? Is it Bonn?'

'Beaune,' Rose replied unable to

suppress a gentle laugh. 'Bonn is a city in Germany.' She looked at the gentlemen opposite them. Mr Pomfret was grinning at Lily indulgently whilst Phillip's eyes were closed again.

* ★ *

The coach entered the outskirts of Beaune a little after seven o'clock that evening. The sun was still shining and everyone peered out of the windows to watch as they approached the walled town which sat on a plain amidst the hills and green vineyards of the Côte-d'Or. They saw the ramparts and battlements of Beaune's city wall first. They looked golden in the evening light.

'What a nice-looking place,' Rose commented. Lily's suggestion of a quick explore the following day was extremely attractive.

The party checked in to a modest but charming inn with a mediaeval style frontage and low beams.

As Mr Pomfret's driver helped Phillip with their suitcases, Rose overhead Mr Pomfret saying he could find them somewhere a bit more luxurious but Rose hoped they'd stay here as she was already a little in love with the place.

After the grandeur of Le Grande Hotel Paris, she was ready for something a bit more homely. The hotel at Auxerre had been richly furnished as well.

Thankfully, Lily, as usual, was 'ravenous' and keen to dress for dinner as soon as possible, so any ideas of changing their accommodation were swiftly abandoned.

★　★　★

Rose slept deeply for the first time since they'd arrived in France in the small but comfortable inn room and felt fully refreshed when she awoke to sunbeams peeping through a gap in the window shutters the next day. It was certainly a relief to escape her worries for a blissful ten hours or so. She couldn't even remember any of her dreams.

'It's a marvellous day,' Lily sang over her croissants at breakfast. 'I knew it!'

'Indeed,' Mr Pomfret replied. 'I propose we take you up on that splendid idea, Miss Lily, and go for a walk before continuing on our journey south.' Phillip made no comment but didn't object to the plan.

After they'd finished eating and stepped outside, he stopped for a moment and raised his face to the sun with a half-smile appearing on his face. Rose sensed some fresh air would do him good.

★　★　★

The streets were cobbled and many of the houses had the same mediaeval frontage as the inn. It was certainly very interesting to see somewhere provincial after their stay in Paris.

The whole town reminded Rose of scenes from her book of fairy stories at home that she'd loved so much as a child.

She half expected to see a handsome prince ride in on horseback in search of a fair maiden locked in one of the tall and cylindrical towers that were dotted around the place.

It wasn't long before they came across a pair of remarkable-looking buildings arranged around a stone courtyard. They looked as if they were someone's home and were large in size but not particularly tall.

The buildings also had the most interesting roofs Rose had ever seen. They were covered in terracotta, green and orange glazed tiles which shone in the morning sunlight.

'Oh, these houses are pretty,' Lily remarked, walking up to them. 'Is this a museum or something? Can we have a look round?'

'I don't think so, Miss Lily,' Phillip answered, whilst for once, Mr Pomfret looked blank. 'If I'm right, I believe these are Les Hospices de Beaune, a hospital and alms-house built for the poor and vulnerable dating back to the fifteenth century.'

'Oh, how wonderful!' Rose exclaimed, as she moved a little closer for a better look. She was vaguely aware that Mr Pomfret was now telling Lily about his time at Christ's College in Cambridge and the glorious summer afternoons he'd spent punting on the River Cam. She knew she didn't have long to take everything in before they'd want to move on.

'They really are quite something, aren't they?' Phillip went on. His voice was quieter than Mr Pomfret's drawl but Rose found herself homing in on his words which were more interesting to her than any student escapades in Cambridge.

'They were built in 1452, on the instructions of a chap called Nicolas Rolin. He was the Chancellor for Duke Phillip the Good. They had just come to the end of the rather ghastly Hundred Years War and the majority of the people of Beaune were destitute. The dreaded plague was everywhere, too.

'Rolin felt he had to do something to help and came up with the idea of a hospital that welcomed everyone regardless of their station in life.

'The doors were open to anyone who found themselves in need whether they were disabled, sick, widowed or orphaned. Fallen women in need of shelter didn't face discrimination, either.

'It's one of the oldest examples of historical philanthropy and remains a hospital for all to this day.'

'What an inspiration,' Rose replied. She thought of her life back in London and the poverty she saw there daily, and again of the chiffoniers on the streets of Paris and their desperate searches through other people's waste.

'One day, when my salary increases at the embassy, and I have a little more time for myself, I'd like to establish something in Paris,' Phillip said.

His eyes were glowing with enthusiasm and Rose barely noticed the dark circles round them any more. He looked more alert than she had ever seen him before.

'I was thinking of a place where people could come and eat a hot meal if they have nowhere else to go and perhaps some information about opportunities for work. I could talk to the construction industries and ask them about any labour shortages and then get the message out to those in search of employment.'

'That's an excellent idea!' Rose exclaimed.

'Well, it's merely the stuff of dreams.' Phillip looked quite sheepish, as if he had shared more than perhaps he ought. 'But it's something that plays on my mind a lot, especially when we're off having sumptuous travels such as this.'

'You could have a little school house there, too,' Rose suggested. The dream was rather infectious. 'The children of poorer families could have some free tuition and their parents, too.'

'You know, I'd never thought of that.' Phillip was looking animated again. 'That's a truly splendid idea. I've always thought that the more one learns, the more choices become available.'

As Mr Pomfret and Lily moved them on, once again a curious feeling of something that felt rather bitter-sweet swept over Rose.

★ ★ ★

Even when they were back in the coach, it continued to gnaw at her insides. She closed her eyes as she tried to let the feelings form some kind of sense.

As much as teaching Julia's children would most likely be quite enjoyable, deep down, Rose knew it would never satisfy her need to make a real change to the world. Perhaps that was why the prospect of a move to Brighton was failing to ignite any fire in her heart.

Rose sighed. Phillip's comment about

173

choices had struck a chord, too. Her love of learning had resulted in only one choice for her.

She opened her eyes and was somewhat startled to see that sitting opposite, Phillip appeared to be staring directly at her and for the second time on this journey, their gaze locked.

As, once again, she shyly let her eyes fall, Rose felt a moment of clarity. It came with a sharp thud to her heart. The other reason she was in such a spin of conflicting emotion was that she desperately didn't want this time with Mr Montgomery, or Phillip, as she'd come to think of him now, to come to an end.

Arrival at Last

The coach trundled into the outskirts of Nice a couple of days after they'd left Beaune. They'd broken the journey again at Avignon and though they'd enjoyed a brief look at the Papal Palace and the famous bridge, Phillip was looking forward to a prolonged stay in one place and was thoroughly sick of sitting in the coach.

Night had fallen by the time they reached their hotel so the visual splendour of the French Riviera would have to wait until the following morning.

Everyone was looking forward to a good supper in the comfortable accommodation that Phillip had booked ahead of the trip and then a swift departure to bed. Mr Pomfret, of course, had managed to wangle his own superior room in the same hotel.

The impressive building was painted in white and pink and overlooked the Mediterranean Sea.

Phillip couldn't wait to open the shutters the next morning and take in the view. Like Le Grande Hotel in Paris, the rooms were furnished with all the opulence and luxury of Second Empire France. The seats in Phillip's room were upholstered in a burgundy coloured velvet and the curtains on the four poster bed were a rich myrtle green. A still life painting of fruit and flowers hung above the ornate fireplace.

Phillip was happy he had picked such a pleasant hotel and hoped the sisters were happy with their rooms, too.

A letter was waiting for Phillip in the hotel lobby when they arrived. He sat down to read it in his room once everyone had retired for the night.

Tuesday 4th May
12 Kensington Church Street.
My dear son Phillip,
    I do hope this finds you all well

and enjoying your travels round France. How did the Misses Banister find the exhibition? I have certainly been thinking of you all. As for me, I am very slowly recovering and feeling a little better every day.

Dear Sally is doing all she can for me and has been the most wonderful nurse. I even managed to sit downstairs for a short while yesterday and enjoyed looking out at the garden. The sweet peas are coming into bloom now and really do look delightful.

Naturally I'm missing you, though it doesn't feel so very different to you being away at the embassy. I do look forward to your return to London, though, of course, it won't be long then till you return to work.

Your father and I are hoping there may be some good news to report once the trip has finished. We are so thrilled by the prospect of welcoming Miss Lily to the family! I can't tell you how happy I feel for you, Phillip, really I can't.

I must stop now as I can hear Sally coming upstairs with my tray of tea.

Safe travels, dearest.

Your loving Mama.

Phillip set the paper down and gave a deep sigh. His body felt exhausted and more than ready for a long night's sleep but his brain was now whirring in such a flurry of activity that he knew that even attempting to rest was impossible.

The letter from his mother was an acute reminder of how much things had changed since he set off with the Banister sisters from London.

Barely a fortnight had passed but he felt worlds away from that excited young man who had burst into his mother's sitting-room with news of a possible courtship.

Pomfret's insistence on dismembering all his meticulous plans had been unwelcome to put it mildly, but Phillip was now feeling very ill at ease by other matters too. His rival had hit a raw nerve by suggesting that Phillip was more interested in Miss Rose than Miss Lily and he had barely been able to rest ever since.

He paced the floor of his room, running over the events of the trip so far in his head. He felt as if he had aged twenty years in only a matter of days. He saw now that the striking beauty in Lily which had so utterly bewitched him on their first few meetings had all but evaporated into the fresh spring air.

He was fond of her, but if he was honest, her incessant chatter bored him to distraction at times. They had no interests in common, either.

The extent of his naivety had hit him full strength in the face on their last evening in Paris and the pain from the blow had been throbbing ever since.

An awful sense of guilt invaded every fibre of his being and he felt he had let everyone down. He had unwittingly brought an innocent young woman to the attention of a ruthless predator.

Anything else he might be feeling had to be put on hold for now. Perhaps now was the time to sit Miss Lily down and tell all he knew about her charming Mr Pomfret?

The pain would be intense but momentary — better by far than discovering the truth too late. Yet the idea of doing so and inevitably ending the holiday was hardly appealing. And igniting the wrath of Pomfret would most likely mean the end of his job at the embassy, too.

The horrible dilemma whirled around Phillip's head as eventually he fell into an uneasy and fitful sleep.

It was populated by weird dreams of Lily in a flowing white gown, dancing gracefully off a high cliff and into a sea of swimming wolves who howled long and hard into the night, whilst Phillip cried powerlessly as he tried in vain to save her.

★   ★   ★

Phillip pulled open the shutters the next day to reveal the wide seafront and for a moment his concerns were forgotten. The sea was a brilliant shade of green, almost azuline, the colour Lily was so taken with at the moment.

Gentle waves lapped against the pebbly shore. It was easily the most beautiful beach that Phillip had ever seen.

Early morning walkers were already out and about. Some had neat little dogs with them. The folk of Nice looked almost as elegant as the Parisians.

He gazed towards the horizon. There was one steamship in sight. Staring out at the expanse of the sea offered a little perspective on Phillip's worries and he resolved to look up and outwards the next time he felt overwhelmed by anxiety again.

* * *

For once Phillip was first down to breakfast and he enjoyed a quiet coffee and croissant for a pleasant ten minutes before Lily's squeals could be heard floating down the hotel corridors.

'This is a dream come true,' she announced as she and Rose took their seats for breakfast. 'We've only ever been to the seaside once when we went with Papa to Margate. Our mother refused to come.'

Lily had abandoned her new love of bright colours for once and was wearing a pale pink cotton dress with a square neckline and flounced sleeves.

She looked almost childlike in the pale pastel colours and Phillip felt his heart ache a little for her as he saw her face light up as Pomfret arrived at the table.

'By Jove, it's unlike me to be last down to breakfast,' he said, as he signalled to the waitress for coffee. 'Hope you're all ready for your first day in Nice.

'I've sent a telegram to the dear friends I mentioned before. They are Lord Cuthbert Bonneville and his wife,

Lady Anne. They're holidaying in their summer residence here until August and would be delighted to meet us for a picnic luncheon later today.'

'Oooh, I've never met a lord before,' Lily cried. 'How wonderfully exciting!'

'Well, he's actually an earl and his wife a countess,' Pomfret replied. 'But Lord and Lady are the titles one uses.'

'You'll have to be on your best behaviour,' Rose added, though she was smiling, too. 'Remember to address them as Lord and Lady Bonneville. It would be most improper to do otherwise.'

Rose was dressed for the summer too in a sky blue cotton gown with a white silk sash round the middle. Phillip noticed how the low tone of her voice calmed him, whilst the high-pitched notes of Lily had profoundly the opposite effect.

★　★　★

After breakfast was finished, the party set off to explore the city of Nice, starting with a stroll along the pebble beach right outside their hotel.

The sun and sea breeze felt gentle on their faces and the air held the salty smell of the sea. The relief of staying in one place for some time was immense and no-one missed the jolts of Pomfret's coach.

Phillip and Rose watched as Lily skipped delightedly along the beach. The pink ribbons in her bonnet danced in the wind. She paused every minute or so to pick up a shell or pebble and examine it closely before throwing it back on the ground.

'She never stops,' Rose said quietly to Phillip as they walked together. At times Lily moved so fast that she looked rather like a pink seabird from the tropics. Pomfret was doing his best to keep up with her but even he struggled a bit, such was her pace.

'She's always several steps ahead of me.' Phillip listened as Rose opened up about the amount of time she spent following Lily and how she was mostly left to pick up the pieces in the aftermath of her younger sister's scrapes.

'As an only child, I had to be content largely with my own company,' Phillip remarked. 'I always envied my friends from large families but I suppose it does have its perks, in that I don't have any siblings to worry about now.'

'Yes, as much as Lily can be exasperating at times, I can't imagine life without her. I mean, I know the day has to come, but, well, I try not to think about it really.' Rose's voice trailed off and they fell into silence.

Phillip knew how highly the sisters regarded each other, even if they didn't always shout very loudly about it.

A fresh pang of guilt swept over him as he watched Pomfret point out a new shell to Lily and heard her whoop of delight as she bent down to pick it up.

Miss Rose would feel her sister's hurt as acutely as her own, if his worst fears came true. His dilemma was whirling round his head once again as they walked on in silence. Suddenly he felt as if the sea breeze held something of a sinister chill as he gave a shudder of unease.

Grave Misgivings

The party walked up the famous Promenade des Anglais and into the city itself to have a look round before heading back to the beach to meet Pomfret's friends for the luncheon picnic that had been arranged. They all enjoyed peering down the intriguing alleyways of the Old Town.

Phillip wasn't hugely looking forward to the introduction to the earl and countess. He disliked formal occasions as a general rule. Moreover, he had met Pomfret's titled friends before and had always felt like an outsider.

The landed gentry and aristocrats seemed to sense his common origins in the much the same way his mother picked out good-hearted people and chose her close friends accordingly. Either that or Pomfret warned them beforehand that 'Old Monty was a shopkeeper's lad.' Phillip wouldn't put it past him at all.

The earl and countess were polite and gracious enough, however, as they greeted the party. They had a small army of servants with them who had laid out a carpet of soft warm blankets and were assembling a vast feast.

There were roast chickens, roast beef and a leg of lamb as well as game pie, boiled potatoes and cold green beans cooked in butter. Glasses of pink lemonade were distributed, too. For pudding, there were fruit turnovers, steamed puddings and tall blancmanges in a rainbow of bright colours.

The midday sun beat down and a couple of purple umbrellas with fancy tassels hanging from them had been placed in the pebbles to prevent any damage from the heat.

'We rather like bringing a bit of home away with us to Nice,' the countess commented as she settled into one of the six wicker chairs that the servants had carried down to the beach.

'Cuthbert can't stand any type of foreign food. We even bring our cook from Kent along with us. Personally I love French cuisine though naturally don't get a say in the matter.'

Phillip wasn't feeling particularly hungry but accepted a plateful of food nonetheless and pretended to busy himself with it but in reality, he was simply cutting up the meat and moving it around the plate.

He looked at everyone else. Lily had been presented with her plate of food and was tucking in whilst nodding politely to something the earl was saying. For once it would seem that she had listened to her older sister. Either that or she was enjoying the food so much that it had momentarily distracted her from any impulsive behaviour.

Rose was quiet, too, though she hadn't eaten much of her big plate of food, either. Although Pomfret appeared to be trying to engage her in conversation, her eyes were focused on one of the earl and countess's servants.

Phillip followed her gaze. She was a very young-looking slip of a girl dressed in the usual white dress of a French servant and a frilly cap, too. There was something in her expression that suggested a melancholy disposition and her thin cheeks had a distinct look of hunger about them.

Phillip could read Rose's face like a book. To sit here consuming such a lavish feast seemed almost criminal in the face of such obvious hardship.

It wasn't long before Rose discreetly pulled out a few pocket handkerchiefs and began placing a couple of potatoes and a few cuts of meat in each one.

Phillip politely averted his eyes. He felt minded to do the same but it would be rather improper for two of the earl's four guests to hoard food in this manner.

He looked around at everyone else, once again. The countess was chatting with Pomfret who had now given up on Rose and they were discussing Kent life back home. It was something to do with the building of some houses on the Bonnevilles' land.

Phillip couldn't help but notice that the earl kept trying to join the conversation and seemed to want to add something about land tax, but the countess seemed determined to ignore him.

After a while the earl gave up and turned his attention back to Lily and the buzz of chatter continued as more refreshments were enjoyed by most of the party and the sun shone on.

'Here, please take it,' Rose was saying in French. Her voice was hushed but Phillip could hear her nevertheless. She was trying to give one of her food parcels to the little maid.

'Thank you, mademoiselle, but no,' the girl whispered in reply.

'Oh, Rose.' Lily's face had crumpled in embarrassment. She opened her mouth to speak further but then presumably had second thoughts and shut it again.

Phillip looked at their hosts. He could tell by the way they were both pointedly looking out to sea that they had seen what Rose was doing.

As the servants began packing up the picnic, the countess began talking loudly about how their 'dear little Aurelie' was naturally a petite young girl.

'Cook has been worried about her too and will insist on giving her the juiciest cuts of the joints, but nothing has worked thus far and she's still a waif of a thing.'

Phillip could only hope the countess was telling the truth. He knew by the look on Rose's face that she was sceptical but nothing more was said on the matter.

*   *   *

'Gracious, Rose,' Lily burst out once they had bid farewell to the Bonnevilles and were making their way back to the hotel. 'And you have the cheek to warn

192

me about correct behaviour in company!'

'That young lady was hungry,' Rose answered stubbornly. 'My conscience wouldn't let me sit back and do nothing.'

'Well, I don't suppose they'll invite us to anything else again,' Lily said, clearly still furious. 'I'm ever so sorry, Mr Pomfret.'

'No harm done, I'm sure,' he replied easily. Phillip was fairly sure he had found the whole thing quite amusing.

Feeling irritated, Phillip drew back from the rest of the group and watched as they walked on ahead. Lily was still talking animatedly and eventually Rose stopped trying to argue with her.

The events of the picnic were fading from Phillip's mind, however. He was more concerned by the fact that Pomfret had placed his hand on the small of Lily's back, presumably to steady her when she'd become impassioned but he was showing no sign of taking it away.

Phillip took a deep breath. He knew that the time for action had come.

A Huge Shock

Lily was quiet and sulky with Rose for several hours after the picnic. Rose had never known her sustain such a silence. Part of her was quite glad of the respite but they hardly ever quarrelled like this and after a while she felt rather uncomfortable.

'Lily, I'm truly sorry I showed you up,' she began once they had retired to their room after dinner that evening. Rose certainly didn't want them to go to bed upset with each other.

'We may have just lost our chance to ever enter high society again,' Lily murmured as she brushed out her locks of blonde hair. It looked like a golden cascade. 'Word spreads you know, Rose.'

'I may have lost that opportunity, yes,' Rose said carefully. She didn't mention that this loss didn't actually concern her very much at all. 'But I've noticed how Mr Pomfret looks at you, Lily, and if I'm right, I don't suppose there will be any shortage of exciting invitations coming up for you in the not so distant future.'

'You think he has formed an attachment to me?' Lily spun round. She didn't look so sulky any more.

'Why, yes, I do,' Rose said.

'Isn't he the most marvellous of men?' Lily's face broke into her bewitching wide smile and she sparkled with happiness. Her poor humour had melted in a heartbeat.

Rose wished she had raised the topic before and saved herself the cold shoulder she had received all evening. Lily's admiration for Mr Pomfret was clear, yet the sisters had yet to discuss their new acquaintance in any serious level of detail.

'He certainly knows how to make an impression,' Rose agreed as she reclined on her bed. 'I must say I was a little worried at first. Phillip didn't seem to take too kindly to him joining us. I mean, Mr Pomfret has rather changed everything, hasn't he?'

'Yes,' Lily replied as she sat down on her bed as well. 'I did feel a little guilty in the beginning, too. It was ever so generous of Phillip to invite us on this trip, of course.

'But it was very early in our courtship really and, you know, I don't think we're very well suited after all. He isn't interested in any of the things I like and sometimes I get the feeling I bore him.

'He loves books, history and social causes, which don't really mean anything to me.' Lily paused and looked over at Rose, a strange expression had appeared on her face.

'I have noticed that you two get on rather well, Rose. I do believe you quite like him.'

'We do have some enjoyable conversations,' Rose answered. She could feel the heat rising up her neck and couldn't quite stop a little smile from creeping across her face.

'I knew it!' Lily squealed joyfully as both sisters dissolved into giggles. 'Who would have guessed it? I go off to France courting one diplomat and come away enamoured with another, whilst it turns out that my very own sister was destined to be with the first diplomat all along!'

Lily was on her feet now and was twirling around on the spot, and Rose, too, felt the room begin to spin with the dizzying realisation that everything might just be falling into place.

Under normal circumstances, Rose would have been quick to remind Lily that nothing had been agreed yet and would have pointed out the perils of getting ahead of oneself, but this once she found herself swept along with this most fairy-tale turn of events.

Finally the prospect of there being a happy ending on the horizon for both the Banister sisters didn't seem quite so many miles away.

The relief of admitting her feelings for Phillip was remarkable and to learn that Lily's heart lay elsewhere felt better still. It was as if a heavy burden had been lifted from her chest.

Rose had thought she was condemned to admire Phillip for ever in silence whilst she tried desperately to convert her love for him to the type one might feel for a brother.

The realisation that this might not in fact be the case brought happy tears to her eyes. It was hard to describe how she felt when Phillip was around. It was as if, for the first time in her life, she'd found someone who truly understood her and listened properly when she opened her mouth.

His brown eyes were full of stories and she loved how they glowed when he spoke of matters close to his heart. Rose had always shared her family's view that her love of books and her attempts to help others in the small ways she could were quirks particular to her and wouldn't ever be shared by anyone else.

To meet someone who didn't raise

their eyebrows in confusion when she spoke of her passions was like a sip of the most delicious cool drink imaginable whilst walking through an endless hot desert.

Lily was still talking as Rose brushed out her hair, too, and got herself ready for bed, but she barely took in anything her younger sister said.

All she could think of was Phillip. The hope that her feelings for him might be reciprocated was all consuming now. The heady bliss of accepting her love was peppered with the tiny seeds of fear that always come when one puts their soul on the line.

Sleep was slow to come but when it did, Rose found that the kindness of Phillip's expressive brown eyes and the warmth of his smile were woven into the very fabric of her dreams.

* * *

Rose felt her hands shake a little the following morning as she busied herself with getting ready for breakfast. The cotton of her day dress felt unusually rough against her skin and her corset seemed tighter than normal, too. It was as if all her senses had awoken and were now acutely sensitive to the world outside.

Lily was chattering away as normal and the noise seemed to thud extra loudly through Rose's head and before long her ears were ringing with Lily's high-pitched cries. Once the sisters were ready, Rose felt her legs shake with every step they took downstairs to the breakfast room.

Rose felt almost paralysed with shyness about seeing Phillip that morning. The voicing of her feelings to Lily had changed the easy dynamic she had felt before.

She was certain he would take one look at her flushed face and darting eyes and instantly know everything. All she could do was keep on praying that he might feel something for her too.

Phillip, however, looked tired and

distracted when he appeared at the breakfast table and barely spoke to either of the sisters as the waitress poured him coffee. He declined all offers of food.

Rose wasn't sure what to make of his demeanour and found that she wasn't able to eat much of her croissant either or the fresh fruit that was on the table. Her mind was a whirl of activity and despite only just having got up for the day, she suddenly felt exceptionally tired.

'Morning all!' came the bright and confident tones of Mr Pomfret. 'It's such a beautiful day that I took a stroll first thing to watch the sunlight sparkle on the sea. It's wonderfully warm already, you know.'

'We must make haste and enjoy it then,' Lily said, sipping quickly at her hot chocolate.

'Oh, and dear Cuthbert has already been in touch by telegraph,' Mr Pomfret continued. 'We are all invited for dinner at their house, Vue Claire, this evening. It's a grand place over-looking the sea with the most wonderful garden. It has several lawns packed full with flowers as well as tennis courts and a croquet lawn.'

'Clear View,' Rose translated the house name quietly to herself. It seemed rather appropriate for all she had experienced in the last few hours.

'How perfect,' Lily answered happily. 'It's good to know your antics with the food hasn't put them off entirely, Rose. We appear to have a second chance.'

'Splendid,' Mr Pomfret replied, just as Phillip cleared his throat.

'Actually, I'm afraid I will need to decline,' he said. Some colour had risen in his face and his voice sounded high-pitched and clipped again, like it had when he had first called on the Banisters on that sunny March day.

'Oh, that's a shame,' Mr Pomfret said, sounding puzzled. 'Would you object if I take the ladies in your absence? I wouldn't want them to miss out too.'

'Actually, the Misses Banister won't be able to attend, either,' Phillip continued, looking even more uncomfortable and refusing to meet anyone's eye. 'There is something in particular that I would like to discuss with you ladies and tonight would be a good time to do so, especially if you intend to accept the invitation and go alone, Pomfret.'

'Can't we discuss it now?' Lily sounded put out as well as bewildered, whilst Rose felt her chest tighten with a sensation she couldn't quite describe.

'I'm afraid not,' Phillip answered with a polite but firm edge to his voice. 'Now if you will excuse me, I'm off to take the morning air.' He stood up abruptly and left the breakfast room without looking back.

Rose thought she had seen an apologetic expression sweep across his face as he rose from his chair but it was so fleeting that she might have been mistaken.

The three of them sat in a haze of

confusion as they tried to finish off their breakfast.

Mr Pomfret made somewhat forced sounding jovial conversation but Rose barely heard him and Lily seemed distracted, too. Clearly neither of them had expected such a strange turn of events.

★   ★   ★

The day continued to feel pretty uncomfortable. Phillip rejoined them after his morning stroll and they all took a trip to Castle Hill where a fortress used to stand.

The panoramic views of Nice were just as impressive as the views from Montmartre with the added bonus of the Mediterranean Sea to admire as well. As beautiful as it all was, Rose struggled to truly appreciate it and though she made the effort to exchange pleasantries with the others, the day passed in something of a blur.

'Whatever do you suppose this is

about?' Lily whispered to Rose at one point when both the gentlemen were out of earshot. Rose could only shrug.

She was as curious as Lily as to what Phillip might have meant and something told her that it wasn't good news.

Lily was unusually quiet for the remainder of their outing and made a point of only speaking directly to Mr Pomfret and her sister. Rose could tell that Phillip had upset her and the mystery surrounding the matter he wished to discuss was only making things worse.

They arrived back at the hotel quite late in the afternoon and Lily promptly announced she was tired and would partake of a lie down. When Rose went to follow her to her room, however, Lily quickly shooed her away.

'Go out and enjoy the rest of the sunshine, Rose,' she said. 'Don't bother yourself with tired little me.'

Rose paused. This was fairly unusual behaviour for Lily but the beach looked wonderfully inviting.

Phillip had swiftly departed to his own room whilst Mr Pomfret had murmured something about dressing for dinner and taken his leave, too. The opportunity to gain a little peace was too tempting to let go and with a promise to return to her sister shortly, Rose took herself off for a quiet walk along the coast.

*   *   *

The crunch of the pebbles was soothing under her feet and for a while Rose lost herself in the crash of the waves and the cries of the seagulls as they swooped and dived overhead.

It helped clear her mind of all the tense curiosity that had built up over the day and staring out at the horizon offered a sense of perspective which was quite unlike any other that Rose had experienced before.

The early evening sunshine was still bright as it glinted on the water and the rays felt warm on Rose's face as the pressures on her mind dissolved in the soft air.

It was only the cry of a young woman summoning her children to dinner that woke Rose from her restful daze.

She had quite lost track of time. She could have spent a lot longer in the gentle evening light but knew Lily would be wondering where she was and would most likely be keen to get the impending discussion with Phillip underway.

Rose was curious, too, but found herself procrastinating a little on her return to the hotel. The trip so far had been dreamlike and she had experienced life in a way she never had before.

Combined with her new-found feelings for Phillip she was in a multifaceted wonderland of change. Whatever it was Phillip wished to discuss, Rose hoped it wouldn't signify the end of the adventure. She was certain now that she didn't wish to go to Brighton and for more reasons than one.

It was past seven o'clock when Rose returned to the hotel. She presumed that she and Lily would meet Phillip in the lobby and that he would have arranged for them to eat dinner somewhere in Nice. Quickly she made her way up the hotel room.

'Sorry I'm a bit late, Lily,' she started as she opened the door. She stopped. Lily's bed was neatly made but her sister was nowhere to be seen.

'Lily?' Rose called, half expecting her younger sister to pop out from inside the wardrobe shouting 'Boo!'

There was no reply. Trying not to panic, Rose sat down on the bed. There were a number of perfectly innocent explanations for Lily's disappearance.

She might have grown bored waiting for Rose and dressed for dinner without her. Or she might have craved some fresh air, too, and taken a quick walk.

Rose decided that the best thing to do was to busy herself with changing her clothes whilst she waited for Lily, who would no doubt breeze through the door any moment in a flurry of her usual vivacity and noise.

It was only after Rose had fastened her green evening down and went to tidy her hair in the gold rimmed oval mirror on the dressing table that she saw the folded slip of paper. With her insides dipping sharply in a painful lurch, Rose opened the note.

'Rose, dear. I simply must go with Gordon to the Bonnevilles'. I don't think Phillip should be allowed to stop me when he won't even tell us why. You will understand, won't you? Please don't be angry with me!'

Rose put the note in her pocket and lost no time in making her way downstairs to the lobby. Why on earth didn't I guess she'd do this, she thought as she hurried down the corridors, almost tripping up a couple of times in her haste. I should never have left Lily on her own.

'Mr Montgomery,' she gasped when she reached the lobby and saw him waiting for them there.

'Miss Rose, whatever's wrong?' His face creased up instantly in concern.

'It's Lily. She's gone to the Bonnevilles' with Mr Pomfret anyway, without a chaperone. I'm ever so sorry and am not quite sure what to do.'

'Oh, good gracious.' Phillip placed his head in his hands and sunk into a nearby armchair. 'What a confounded mess.'

'Well she's safe enough with Mr Pomfret, but I do worry about them turning up at the Bonnevilles' unchaperoned. Whatever will they think of her?'

'It's an awful lot worse than that, I'm afraid, Miss Rose,' Phillip replied. His head was still in his hands. 'The matter I wanted to discuss with you both tonight is something I really should have raised before and now I fear I have left it too late.'

'Please tell me,' Rose said, trying desperately to keep her voice calm. She sat down in the chair opposite him.

'Mr Pomfret has been secretly

betrothed since childhood,' Phillip blurted out, 'to a Miss Charlotte Marsay in Suffolk. Her parents own a substantial estate there. It's a match both their families have been excited about for some time.

'I fear my colleague is guilty of deceiving your sister and now circumstances have escalated even further and I worry for both her reputation and well-being.'

Rose felt her face turn ashen.

'We need to go and find her,' was all she could say as they rose from their chairs, ran through the lobby and out into the street.

Missing

Conversation was sparse as Phillip and Rose made their way to Vue Claire, the coastal residence of Lord and Lady Bonneville. Thankfully Phillip had a good idea where to find it as the earl had proudly described its perfect seaside location during their picnic the previous day.

Rose's face was very pale, her lips were pursed and she walked with a steely determination.

Whatever must she think of me, Phillip thought as new waves of guilt drenched him again. How could he have put his role at the embassy before Lily? It was terrible, unforgivable in fact.

It was true that Pomfret had rather backed him into a corner but he saw now that he should have aborted the trip in Paris when Pomfret announced he would be joining them in Nice.

He wished the whole holiday had never taken place at all. If it were possible to rewind the clock, he would never have stopped to watch that parade in Hyde Park on that Wednesday afternoon which now felt a lifetime ago.

It wasn't long before they reached the Bonnevilles' cliff-side mansion, a four-storeyed monster of a house with gas lanterns on the pillared porch lighting up its façade. The building was constructed of white brickwork and had white painted shutters at each of its many windows. It was certainly an impressive abode. You could almost smell the wealth radiating from it.

Phillip lost no time in striding up to the ornate front door and knocking loudly upon it. It was opened almost immediately by the petite little maid who had come to the picnic. Phillip thought her name was Aurelie.

'Are Monsieur Pomfret and Mademoiselle Banister here?' he asked quickly in French.

'No, sir,' Aurelie answered. 'They did arrive here an hour or so ago but left abruptly at Monsieur Pomfret's insistence. They didn't even stay for dinner.'

Phillip thanked her quickly as panic surged through him.

'We should split up,' Rose said. 'We'll have to search for them but it's impossible to know where to start.' She was as polite as always but Phillip could see something that looked like anger burning in her eyes.

'No,' he replied. The light was fading and ominous dark clouds had appeared in the sky. It was hard to believe rain was coming when the evening had been so pleasant so far and the air was still full of warmth.

'I would prefer to stick together if that is agreeable to you. I would rather not lose another Banister sister tonight.'

Rose said nothing in reply but kept pace with him nevertheless, which he took for acceptance.

'My instinct is to start with the beach,' Rose said eventually and Phillip found himself nodding in agreement. Neither of them spoke of where Pomfret might have taken Lily or what his intentions might be.

As dislikeable as he found the man and as much as he might disagree with his ethics, Phillip found it hard to believe that he might intentionally hurt Lily.

He still suspected that Pomfret held no regard or respect whatsoever for how this scandal would impact on her reputation and her prospects for a future match. The Bonnevilles were bound to talk and Lily was right, word spread.

If there was any decency in Pomfret whatsoever, surely he would put a stop to this absurd charade and tell her the truth himself but evidently he had not chosen to use a moral compass in this reckless and cruel adventure.

The first drops of rain had begun to fall when Phillip and Rose reached the beach. Darkness had fallen now but thankfully a large full moon shone through a gap in the clouds giving them a little light to see by.

'Lily!' Rose called into the darkness, but the only reply was the relentless crash of the waves. They seemed louder than they had in the daytime, perhaps because the seabirds were now roosting for the night or maybe because the tide was drawing in.

They carried on walking for what felt like hours calling out Lily's name from time to time but mostly they stayed silent in the hope that they would be more likely to hear her this way. The rain was light but soon they were wet through.

'This is hopeless, she could be anywhere,' Rose said eventually when they neared some cliffs at the end of the bay. Just then a heavy cloud slipped over the moon and they were plunged into a deep darkness.

Phillip was uncomfortably aware that the tide was even further in as the waves were even louder now, too.

'Perhaps we had better head to the

hotel,' Phillip suggested. 'They might have gone back there.'

'I want to try the city first,' Rose replied. 'I don't suppose it will make any difference but I have to do something otherwise I'll go quite mad.'

'Yes, it's good to stay occupied,' Phillip agreed. Mercifully the rain had stopped which was something. Phillip felt clammy and hot in his wet clothes.

'Miss Rose,' he started as they turned around. He couldn't see her face but had a sense that her eyes were staring hard at him. 'I really am sorry for this most unfortunate turn of events. I can assure you that I never intended for anything like this to happen.'

'Let's just find my sister,' was her reply. Her voice sounded tight and strained. Losing all hope of forgiveness, Phillip gave one last shout for Lily. He heard his voice crack as he did so.

'Over here,' came a reply. Both Rose and Phillip started. It wasn't Lily's voice, that was for sure and though it was most definitely male, it didn't sound like Pomfret's either.

'Where are you?' Phillip called back.

'In the sea,' the voice replied.

'Merciful heavens,' Rose said. Her voice was merely a whisper.

The moon had slipped out of the clouds now to reveal two figures at the shore. Both of them appeared to be in the water though one was far deeper than the other. Without hesitating, Phillip ran over to them. He could hear from her pounding footsteps that Rose wasn't far behind.

'What on earth?' Phillip panted once he got to the water. Pomfret was wading further out into the sea. He had known that the slight figure was his supposed friend from the moment the moon shone down on him. It was only the panic in his cry that had confused him as to who it could be.

'She was looking for shells,' Pomfret replied weakly as Phillip joined him in the water, quickly removing his jacket and shoes.

The water clung to his trousers,

though as they were wet already it didn't make much difference. Still, Phillip shuddered as a rush of cold sea seeped into his skin.

'We just came for a walk on the beach once the rain stopped but I couldn't prevent her going to the water. The tide was closer and stronger than we thought. She can't swim.'

'Enough,' Phillip said as he waded further. He could hear Rose crying at the water's edge and the tiny cries of Lily who had lost her balance. There was clearly a sharp dip in the sand fairly close to shore that meant Lily had been almost instantly thrown out of her depth.

'I'm coming,' he shouted firmly, as once again, he tried to disguise the panic in his voice. It wasn't long before he had lost his depth, too, and was swimming out towards her.

The current was strong and seemed determined to halt his progress.

Phillip wasn't surprised that Lily had been swept away. The sea seemed to be getting colder too and Phillip felt himself shivering and heard his teeth chatter.

Thankfully he reached Lily in time to grab her by the hand and steer them both back to shore. She too was shivering uncontrollably and wasn't even able to speak. He lost her hand at one point and resorted to holding her by the waist instead.

Eventually he was able to touch the sea floor again and the relief of being able to wade to shore was indescribable.

Phillip found himself whispering a prayer of thanks. He was certain a higher power had been looking out for them that night.

As soon as they reached dry land, Rose threw herself at Lily and the sisters clutched each other in a stream of sobs and heavy gasps.

'I thought I'd lost you,' he heard Rose whisper into Lily's wet hair.

'Good job, my man,' Pomfret said, moving over as if to shake his hand but

Phillip wouldn't look at him.

As soon as Lily was able to walk, Phillip led the group home. She still clung to Rose whilst Pomfret followed them in silence. Phillip's wet clothes were making him feel very uncomfortable but that was nothing compared to the way he felt inside. First and foremost, he was incredibly concerned for Lily. It was imperative that she got into some warmth or she might come down with pneumonia.

'It's time for a hot bath and bed,' Rose said briskly by way of goodnight when they reached the hotel. 'Oh — and I think Lily and I should go home in the morning, Mr Montgomery. I'm sure you'll agree, given the circumstances.' Her eyes were bright with tears but her voice was firm.

'Of course,' he answered quietly. 'I was going to suggest the same thing myself.'

'But . . . ' Lily opened her mouth to speak. Her face was patchy with bright red flushes and wet sand had stuck to her sodden dress. A bottle green stem of seaweed had wrapped itself into the tangles of her bedraggled hair.

'Now, Lily,' Rose said as she ushered her sister away before Lily could say any more.

★   ★   ★

The journey home was a tense and uncomfortable affair. Pomfret had offered them his coach but Phillip coolly declined. He asked the hotel to make arrangements for him to hire one of his own.

'Look, old chap, I think we've misunderstood ourselves a bit,' Pomfret had said the following morning when Phillip appeared downstairs with his suitcase.

'You allow an innocent young woman to almost drown and risk goodness knows what to her reputation by taking her into society unchaperoned,' Phillip thundered in reply. 'I don't think there has been any misunderstanding at all!'

'It would appear that way,' Pomfret

replied sheepishly. 'But if you'll only let me explain . . .'

'Save it,' Phillip said tightly. He signalled to the sisters who were waiting by the lobby door that it was time to leave. Lily looked as if she wanted to say something to Pomfret but Rose took her arm and the three of them left the hotel.

★ ★ ★

'Travelling again,' Lily murmured as the coach trundled along the Nice roads. The seats weren't as soft as in Pomfret's coach, either.

'Yes, I'm so sorry the trip didn't go according to plan,' Phillip said. He had never felt so wretched in his life. His body felt a hundred times heavier than usual and every joint ached. Lily looked close to tears whilst Rose shut her eyes. It was going to be a long journey back to Britain.

Back at Upper Wimpole Street

Mrs Banister's face was drawn as she stood in the hallway to receive her daughters on their return to the family home. Mr Banister was waiting quietly in the sitting-room.

'Nell has made some supper for you both,' she told them, rather than saying hello. Both sisters had braced themselves for their mother's fury at the unfortunate ending of the trip.

Rose had written ahead to warn her of their early return home. Mrs Banister, however, didn't raise her voice a single notch, though her face looked drawn, tired and a little older with worry lines on her brow.

Rose almost wished she would shout at them. Her obvious disappointment was close to unbearable. As promised, some boiled ham was waiting for them along with potatoes and carrots.

Rose took a bite of the food but it was merely to satisfy her mother and set a good example to Lily who had barely eaten for days.

Rose had thought the trip home would never end and it was rather depressing to think they had spent more time on a coach than they had done in Nice. That was nothing, however, in comparison to her worries for Lily and her bitter disappointment in their supposed friends.

Rose could barely believe that Phillip could have let that deceitful scoundrel infect their holiday in such an insidious manner, when he had known all along of his secret betrothal to Miss Marsay.

It certainly explained his discontent at Mr Pomfret's arrival, yet why hadn't he steered them away more assertively at the time?

Rose had to concede that the situation would have been rather awkward for Phillip but surely he should have put Lily's safety and her reputation before all that. Perhaps he had left well alone as a means of revenge? After all, Lily had shifted her admiration to his rival. Rose didn't want to believe it of him, but felt she had little choice.

Lily had been inconsolable when Rose gently broke the news to her in their hotel room at Avignon en route back to Calais. They had just endured a tense dinner with Phillip and were getting ready for bed.

'I won't believe it, Rose. I won't!' she sobbed as Rose stroked her back in a fruitless endeavour to comfort her.

'Why on earth did you leave the Bonnevilles' house so early?' Rose asked, when Lily was eventually calm enough to speak again. 'Aurelie told us that you didn't even stay for dinner.'

'Gordon insisted,' Lily said, in between sniffs. 'It was a bit strange there, to be honest. The house was so beautiful but we waited in the hallway for about twenty minutes before Lady

Anne appeared and when she did, she behaved rather oddly. I wondered if she'd been crying as her eyes looked red. Lord Cuthbert was nowhere to be seen. Eventually he came downstairs but he seemed a bit distant too.'

'That does sound rather peculiar,' Rose answered. 'Still, Mr Pomfret had no business disappearing off with you into the night without a chaperone. It was most improper. And what on earth was he thinking taking you down to the beach in the darkness?'

'That was my idea,' Lily replied, her eyes welling up again. 'Gordon said he wished to speak with me on a matter of great importance. We were sheltering from the rain in a shop porch.

'Once it stopped and the moon came out, I insisted that I wanted to search for shells by moonlight. I thought it would be romantic.' Lily dissolved into tears again and Rose had no choice but to stroke her back once more until she cried herself to sleep.

Rose pushed some food around her

plate. The few mouthfuls she'd taken had failed to make her feel any better. She had been so focused on getting Lily home, she had barely stopped to consider her own feelings in all this. Her anger at Phillip was still raw but there was a desperate sadness there, too.

I'm a clumsy fool, she thought to herself as hot tears formed in her eyes. How could she have even supposed that Phillip might feel anything for her other than perhaps a fondness that had grown from the shared experience of travelling together?

Anyone who would disregard Lily in that manner could hardly hold any respect for either of them and he had barely looked at her all the way home.

He is Mr Montgomery to you again now, she told herself firmly though she highly doubted that either she or Lily would ever see the diplomat again.

Rose looked around the Banisters' neat dining-room with the polished oak table, silver candle sticks and wooden wall clock with its brass pendulum swinging back and forth. She could hear her mother giving instructions to Nell in the kitchen next door and a familiar tune was playing on her father's music box in the sitting-room.

It was as if the whole adventure had never taken place.

As Rose thought back to the excitement of the steam ship, the opulence of the Grande Hotel Paris, the assortment of sensations at the exhibition, watching Paris sprawl out from Montmartre hill, her admiration of the Hospices of Beaune and even the jolts of Mr Pomfret's coach, she couldn't help but let a few wistful tears fall.

The most wonderful of dreams had turned into something of a nightmare, yet Rose still found herself wishing she could fall back to sleep.

Lily had shuffled off to her bedroom, Nell had cleared the table and Rose found herself alone. Without further ado she went to find some paper and ink. As despairing as she felt, she knew she should make plans for her future without any further delay. It wouldn't do her any good to stay much longer at Upper Wimpole Street. After all, she wasn't a child any more.

★   ★   ★

'Dear Julia,' she wrote, feeling her fountain pen shake in her hand. 'I believe I have a solution to your dilemma about securing a suitable governess for your children. I am now home from France and find myself in need of employment. I think it would work well for all concerned if I offer my services to you.'

Rose hadn't got much further when there was a knock at the front door. She ignored it. It was most likely a message for one of her parents. She wasn't sure any of her and Lily's friends even knew they were back.

It wasn't long, however, before Rose was aware of some activity around the rest of the house. Nell was racing up the stairs and she could hear both her parents talking in the hallway. They were inviting someone indoors. Next she heard the polite tones of a voice she knew very well.

'Mr Pomfret is here,' came the voice of her father. He too looked strained and his expression was hard to read. Rose had spared her parents most of the torrid details in her letter but had been frank that an unsuitable attachment had formed between Lily and this gentleman.

'Goodness,' she cried. The shock to her body was acute and she felt her hands shaking again.

'He has requested a formal meeting with Lily,' Mr Banister replied.

'He doesn't know when to stop.' Rose felt a sickening panic rise in her throat. 'He must leave the house at once.'

'Well, I did ask him about his intentions,' Mr Banister said. 'I thought it was more than fair given the circumstances. And, the truth is, Rose, he asked me for permission to propose to Lily and explained that he loves her to distraction.' Rose gasped and the pen she was holding dropped to the floor. Her father's face broke into a smile. 'He's talking to her now.'

'But . . . ' Rose started, only to be interrupted by a thud of the front door and the sound of Lily's musical laugh echoing around the hallway. She and her father left the dining-room to find Lily and Mr Pomfret being ushered into the sitting-room by Mrs Banister.

'We're engaged!' Lily announced, brandishing an expensive-looking diamond sitting atop a golden ring.

'She's supposed to wait till we formally announce it before she wears the ring,' Mr Pomfret explained, 'but naturally Lily finds that impossible.'

He looked different somehow in the Banister's sitting-room. There was no sun to lighten his golden blond hair and his smile was humbler, too. The aura of importance had left him and he looked a little nervous. He had dressed conservatively for once in a brown tailored suit and white shirt.

'He was going to ask me that night in Nice, but I spoiled it by insisting on walking to the beach and then getting into a spot of trouble,' Lily trilled.

Rose tried not to smile. This euphemistic version of events was faintly similar to that fateful slip in the mud all those weeks ago.

'What about Miss Marsay?' Rose asked.

'If you will allow me to explain . . . ' Mr Pomfret's voice was hurried and his face looked a little flushed which was highly unusual for him.

'I was betrothed to Miss Charlotte, yes, but it was a decision made by our parents when we were very young and we really didn't have any say in the matter at all.' He cleared his throat.

'I must confess that my conduct has been somewhat questionable in the past and Phillip Montgomery was quite justified in his concerns. But Miss Rose, Mr and Mrs Banister, please believe me when I tell you that I love your Lily with all of my heart.

'She has made me smile every day that I have known her and is delightful in all her quirks and stumbles. I just had to come back to London to find her and though I looked out for you on the steamship, it would seem I took a different boat.

'It was when we were sitting in Lord and Lady Bonneville's large and ornate sitting-room that I had a realisation that, although they have the best money can buy, they have no love for each other at all. And that is what's truly priceless. I will brave the wrath of my family for Lily's hand in marriage. I cannot lose happiness like this.'

Lily's eyes were brimming with happy tears and Rose felt hers well up again too. She had thought they'd be cried out now but somehow there was always room for more.

'Monty and I are friends again too. I've just come from his house now where he gave me your address.

'Once I explained my intentions

towards Lily he forgave me for rather taking over his holiday with you ladies. I know that I can be a bit of an oaf at times and I apologised for that too. Monty has even agreed to be best man at our wedding. Fancy that!'

Rose sat quietly as the joy of her family whirled round her and marvelled at how a single knock on the door had the power to change everything.

The celebratory atmosphere felt very much like that day in March when Phillip first called on the Banister sisters. Who knew then what lay ahead?

Rose tried not to dwell on her memories. Lily was engaged to a man of high social standing. It was a better match than the Banisters had ever dreamed possible.

At least one of us got it right, Rose thought as she slipped out of the room. It had been an exceptionally long day and she needed to lie down.

Wedding Bells

The following weeks were a flurry of activity. Lily was in a turbulent spin of excitement and nervous energy as she prepared for her wedding. It was to take place during mid-July in the Banisters' local church.

It seemed that Mr Pomfret's family had accepted the match though clearly it had never been their plan. He had extended his leave from the embassy to allow for the wedding and the happy couple would return to France together once the marriage ceremony had taken place.

Meanwhile Rose was busy, too. Julia had written to accept her offer of governess and was delighted to welcome Rose into her household. It was an 'altogether perfect solution', she wrote back.

As Julia and Bartholomew were to

attend Lily's wedding now that their new baby had arrived and was in Martha's care, it was agreed that Rose would then accompany them back to Brighton to start her new life.

'I'll lose two daughters in the same day,' Mrs Banister had murmured. The difference in their fortunes had never been more striking. Lily was marrying a successful diplomat who was heir to a huge estate. She would be living in Paris and mixing with the most fashionable people in the highest society. Rose, on the other hand, was effectively becoming a servant.

'You don't need to go,' Mrs Banister had told her when Rose explained her plan. 'Now that Lily has such a favourable match, you can stay here with us. We would like that very much.'

'Thank you, Mama.' Rose was genuinely touched. 'But I must be occupied. I'll go quite mad if I've nothing to do. I'll enjoy the teaching, I'm sure.'

Amidst packing, planning lessons and

trying to stay patient when Lily asked her opinion on wedding flowers for probably the 20th time, Rose was generally successful in her endeavours to keep her mind from Phillip. It was only at night, when she was trying to sleep that she struggled to stop herself thinking of him.

She had half dared to hope that Mr Pomfret's proposal and the revelation that he was an honourable gentleman after all might prompt Phillip to at least visit the sisters, but no such call had been made. To go from seeing him every day to no contact at all was hard.

Rose wasn't sure if he had returned to Paris already or was still in London. She couldn't help but keep a hopeful eye out for him whenever she left the house and particularly when she walked in Hyde Park.

Although she mistook several strangers momentarily for him, her walks always ended in disappointment.

Rose knew she would see him at the wedding itself and the thought made her breathless with angst. How bitter-sweet it would be to watch the man she'd grown to love help his friend marry her sister and smile politely as if he were no more than a passing acquaintance.

She tried to appear jolly in mood as she watched Lily prepare for the happiest day of her life but a painful jealousy gripped her all the same. At times it was utterly unbearable.

★　★　★

The day of the wedding was bright and clear. The sunbeams felt warm on Phillip's face as he made his way over to St Mary's, the Marylebone parish church where Gordon and Lily were to marry.

He was feeling more than a little nervous as he walked the familiar route from Kensington to Marylebone, stopping as he had done before at the flower stall in Marble Arch. After all, one couldn't turn up to a wedding without a bouquet of flowers.

Phillip had been ready to slam the door in Gordon Pomfret's face when he turned up on his doorstep, barely an hour after he himself had arrived home from France.

'I have to explain, Phillip, really I do,' he had said over and over again. Phillip wasn't sure if it was the fact that Gordon had used his first name for once or that he'd followed him straight back from Nice, but he ended up listening to his explanation.

It wasn't until after he had watched Gordon write to his family to inform them that he wished to release Miss Marsay from their betrothal and had walked with him to the post office himself to see him post the letter that Phillip could even start to believe that his old rival might actually be telling the truth.

'I must say that I'm a little taken aback by your hostility to me, old fellow,' Gordon had said once they were back in the Montgomery's house. 'I'd thought that despite the odd clash at work, we were actually quite good chums.

'I'm sorry if I can be a bit of a show-off at times and I know you don't always take to my other friends but I really would be quite happy if we could make something of a truce, especially now you know that my intentions towards Miss Lily are nothing if not honourable.'

Phillip found himself taking Gordon's outstretched hand and felt a moment of connection as he nodded.

Perhaps he was a little guilty of harbouring old resentments from their school days and seeing only the worst in his colleague. He wasn't sure they would ever be the best of friends but, still, it was a relief to say goodbye to all that animosity and unpleasantness. He was genuinely happy to accept Gordon's invitation to be best man at the wedding.

The following weeks had passed in a blur as, after a slow but steady recovery, his mother suddenly fell ill again as a fresh bout of pneumonia struck.

Phillip vowed that he wouldn't leave her side this time and applied for an extension of his holiday from the embassy. He spent his time reading, talking and playing tunes from their music box to his mother and found that the distraction was really quite welcome.

He couldn't help but turn his thoughts to Rose though and often wondered what she might be doing and what her plans for the future were now.

He wasn't sure she would ever forgive him for his part in the creation of that dense and tangled web of misunderstandings that had spoiled their holiday in France, despite the happy ending for Lily.

Every time he thought of that tight look on her face as they searched, or the panic in her cry as she called for her younger sister, a new surge of guilt powered through him and he had to focus on something else to take the pain away.

★ ★ ★

Before he knew it the big day had arrived and Phillip felt his heart beating hard as he opened the churchyard gate.

'Monty! Thank goodness you're here!'

Gordon rushed over to him in a whirlwind of last minute instructions and a long list of tasks. Phillip could feel the nervous energy pouring off him and found it was pretty infectious, too.

He patted his pocket more than a few times to make sure the wedding ring was still there and found a safe place to leave the flowers. He wouldn't need them just yet.

Phillip had to smile when he saw the floral decorations. The whole church was full of bright red roses combined with delicate white lilies. Their gentle scent floated round the whole of the building. He could hear the guests murmuring how the choice of flowers was a perfect way to celebrate both the Banister sisters.

Next, it was time for Phillip and Gordon to stand by the altar and wait. Naturally, Lily was several minutes late. Phillip wouldn't have expected anything less.

When the bridal march began and she entered, Phillip took a sharp intake of breath. In her flowing silken gown with delicate white lace on the bodice and a long sheer cotton veil, Lily was utterly captivating.

He glanced at her parents who for once had abandoned their polite façade and were glowing with pride and happiness. Mrs Banister wiped tears from her cheeks.

Gordon's eyes looked bright too as he took in his beautiful bride. Phillip fully appreciated then how perfect they were for each other.

Phillip was aware that Rose was standing behind Lily as her maid of honour. He could feel her eyes on him as the ceremony went on but found himself unable to look at her directly as a deep and shameful heat rose up from his chest. He'd never felt so unworthy or so small.

After the ceremony, the wedding moved on to the Banisters' house where a sumptuous luncheon had been laid out on long trestle tables in their back garden which was packed full of blossoming and sweet scented summer flowers.

Phillip found himself unable to eat a thing, however, as he watched the other guests enjoying themselves in the glorious sunshine. He had picked up the bouquet and now held it in his hands. He had chosen roses, too, but the pink dusky variety rather than the vibrant bright red of the church flowers.

'I'm sorry to leave so early, but we really must make haste to Brighton,' he heard a familiar voice say to a guest standing close by. 'I start my new job there as a governess today, you know.'

'Miss Rose,' he said quickly, neither

wanting nor caring to find the right time any more. She looked up, startled, and gave him a questioning look.

She was wearing a flowing white gown too but without the lace detail of Lily's and those gentle curls fell gracefully around her wide-eyed face.

'I beg your pardon,' Phillip went on, 'but I simply must speak with you very urgently.'

'Yes, Mr Montgomery?' she asked formally as they walked to the end of the garden. Phillip placed the bouquet of flowers in her hands.

'Miss Rose, I should have brought you flowers long ago. I don't know if you can ever forgive me for the series of unhappy events that unfolded abroad,' Phillip started. 'I also don't know if you'll forgive me for being so absent ever since we returned,' he continued.

'My mother fell sick again but truth be told I'm something of a coward and didn't quite know how to approach you. I entreat you, Rose, if I may call you by your first name, please do not leave for Brighton today.'

'But . . . ' she started, glancing back to the wedding guests.

'I'm entirely in love with you,' Phillip blurted out in a rush of emotion, 'and have been for some time. I can only hope that you might feel the same way.' He paused as he tried to assess the expression on her upturned face. Her eyes were brimming with tears.

'I felt in France as if I had found another me,' she whispered. 'Does that make any sense?'

'It makes perfect sense, my darling,' Phillip said as he took her hand. 'With you by my side, I would have the strength to take on anything. We could build that shelter for those in need, the one I spoke with you about in Beaune.'

'And a school,' Rose replied, laughing a little through her tears.

'We'll have to get married first,' Phillip said as he squeezed her hand and drew her a bit closer. 'If you'll have me?'

'I will,' Rose answered softly in reply

as the sun shone on overhead. 'I've never felt so complete.'

We do hope that you have enjoyed reading this large print book.

Did you know that all of our titles are available for purchase?

We publish a wide range of high quality large print books including:
Romances, Mysteries, Classics
General Fiction
Non Fiction and Westerns

Special interest titles available in large print are:
The Little Oxford Dictionary
Music Book, Song Book
Hymn Book, Service Book

Also available from us courtesy of Oxford University Press:
Young Readers' Dictionary
(large print edition)
Young Readers' Thesaurus
(large print edition)

For further information or a free brochure, please contact us at:
Ulverscroft Large Print Books Ltd.,
The Green, Bradgate Road, Anstey,
Leicester, LE7 7FU, England.
Tel: (00 44) **0116 236 4325**
Fax: (00 44) **0116 234 0205**